Sudden
MISCHIEF

ROBERT B. PARKER

BERKLEY BOOKS, NEW YORK

SUDDEN MISCHIEF

A Berkley Book / published by arrangement with
the author

PRINTING HISTORY
G. P. Putnam's Sons edition / March 1998
Berkley edition / May 1999

The Penguin Putnam Inc. World Wide Web site address is
http://www.penguinputnam.com

ISBN: 0-425-16828-X

BERKLEY®
Berkley Books are published by The Berkley Publishing Group,
a division of Penguin Putnam Inc.,
375 Hudson Street, New York, New York 10014.
BERKLEY and the "B" logo are trademarks belonging to
Penguin Putnam Inc.

PRINTED IN THE UNITED STATES OF AMERICA

10 9 8 7 6 5 4 3 2 1

(continued on next page)

For Joan: Gloriana

"Be well aware," quoth then that Ladie milde,
"Least suddaine mischiefe ye too rash provoke"

THE FAERIE QUEENE

One

WE WERE AT the Four Seasons Hotel, in the Bristol Lounge. Bob Winter was playing "Green Dolphin Street" on the piano. I was drinking beer and Susan was doing very little with a glass of red wine. There were windows along the Boylston Street side of the room that looked out on the Public Garden, where winter was over, the swan boats were being cleaned, and had there been a turtledove awake at this hour we'd have almost certainly heard his voice.

"I need a favor," Susan said to me.

Her black hair was shiny and smelled slightly of lavender. Her eyes were impossibly big, and full of intelligence and readiness, and something else. The something else had to do with throwing caution to the winds, though I'd never been able to give it a name. People looked at her when she came in. She had the quality that made people wonder if she were someone important. Which she was.

"You know I'm the only guy in the room knows the lyrics to 'Green Dolphin Street,' " I said, "and you want me to sing them softly to you."

"Don't make me call the bouncer," she said.

"At the Four Seasons? You'd have to tip him before he threw you out."

"It's about my ex-husband," Susan said.

"The geek?"

"He's not a geek," Susan said. "If you knew him, you'd kind of like him."

"Don't confuse me," I said.

Winter played "Lost in Loveliness." The waitress looked at my empty beer glass. I nodded. Susan's glass was still full.

"He came to see me last week," Susan said. "Out of the blue. I haven't seen him in years. He's in trouble. He needs help."

"I'm sure he does," I said.

"He needs help from you."

My second beer came. I thought about ordering a double shot of Old Thompsons to go with it but decided it was more manly to face this moment sober. I drank some of my beer.

"Okay," I said.

"I . . ." She stopped and looked out the windows for a moment. "I guess I'm kind of embarrassed to ask you," she said.

"Yeah," I said. "It is kind of embarrassing."

"But I am going to ask you anyway."

"Who else?" I said.

She nodded and picked up her glass and looked at it for a moment and put it down without drinking.

"Brad is being sued by a group of women who are charging him with sexual harassment."

I waited. Susan didn't say anything else.

"That's it?" I said.

"Yes."

"And what was it you thought I could do about it?"

"Prove them wrong," she said.

"Maybe they're right," I said.

"Brad is on the very edge of dissolution. If he gets dragged into court on this kind of thing . . . he hasn't got enough money to defend himself."

"Or pay me," I said.

Susan nodded. "Or pay yes," she said.

"That's encouraging," I said.

"I don't love him," Susan said. "Maybe I never did. And he hasn't been in my life for years, but . . ."

"But you used to know him and you don't want to see him destroyed."

"Yes."

"And you don't know what else to do, or who else to ask."

"Yes."

"So," I said. "I'll take the case."

"And the fee?"

"If I get him off, you have to ball my socks off," I said.

"And if you don't get him off?"

"I have to ball your socks off."

The something I had no name for flickered in Susan's eyes.

"Sounds fair to me," she said.

"Okay, I'm on the case," I said. "Tell me about him."

"His name is Brad Sterling."

"Sterling?"

Susan looked down at the table.

"He changed it," she said.

"From Silverman. As in sterling silver, how precious."

"How un-Jewish," Susan said.

"How come you kept his name?"

"When we were first divorced I guess it was just easier. It was on my license, my social security card, my checking account."

"Uh huh."

"And I guess it was a way of saying that even if I weren't married, I had been."

"Like a guy wearing his field jacket after he's been discharged."

"Except that the jacket will still keep him warm."

"You wish you'd gone back to your . . . what's the correct phrase these days?"

"Birth name," Susan said.

"Thank you. Do you wish you'd kept your birth name?"

"I suppose so, but by the time I was healthy enough to do that, I was healthy enough not to need to."

"Susan Hirsch," I said.

"Sounds odd, doesn't it."

"Makes me think of sex," I said.

"More than Silverman?"

"No, that makes me think of sex too."

"How about Stoopnagel?"

"Yeah," I said. "That makes me think of sex."

"I think I'm seeing a pattern here," Susan said.

"That's because you're a trained psychologist," I said. "Tell me about Sterling."

"I was a freshman at Tufts," Susan said. "He was at Harvard, my roommate and his roommate were cousins and we got fixed up."

Susan was many things, and almost all of them wondrous, but she was not succinct. I minded this less than I might have, because I loved to listen to her talk.

"He was a tackle on the Harvard football team. The only Jew ever to play tackle in the Ivy League, he used to say. I think he was kind of uneasy being Jewish at Harvard."

I made eye contact with the waitress and she nodded.

"He was very popular, had a lot of friends. Got by in class without studying much. I really liked him. We were married the week after graduation."

"Big wedding?"

"Yes," Susan said. "Have I never talked about this with you?"

"No."

"Didn't you ever want to know?"

"I want to know what you want to tell me."

"Well, I saw no point to talking to you about other men in my life."

"Up to you," I said. "I don't need to know. And I don't need to pretend there weren't any."

She didn't speak for a time. She slowly turned her wine glass by the stem and looked at me as if thinking about things.

"I always assumed it would bother you," she said.

"I'm entirely fascinated with you," I said. "And what you are is a result of what you were, including the other men."

She was quiet again, looking at me, turning her glass. Then she smiled.

"It was a very big wedding at Memorial Chapel at Harvard. Reception at the Ritz."

"Brad's family had money," I said.

"Not after the reception," Susan said. "Actually, Brad's father ran a salvage business in Chelsea. But by the time I came along he'd moved the family to

Wellesley. Brad went to Harvard. His sister went to Bryn Mawr."

The waitress brought me another beer. Susan took a sip of her wine. Racing to catch up.

"Then what?" I said.

"Then not much," Susan said. "His father bought us a little house in South Natick."

"Just across the line from Wellesley."

"Yes. Brad's mother was ten minutes away on Route 16."

"Perfect."

"And Brad got a job with an advertising agency in town."

"You?"

"I stayed home and wore cute aprons and redid my makeup every afternoon before he came home for supper."

"Supper?"

Susan smiled.

"I know," she said. "It was pathetic. I couldn't cook. I didn't want to learn. I hate to cook."

"Is that so," I said.

"The house was a four-room Cape with an unfinished attic. I could stand in the hall and see all four rooms."

"You can do that now," I said. "In your apartment."

"Yes, but I live there alone."

"Except for Pearl," I said.

"Pearl is not a person," Susan said.

"Try telling her that."

"I hated the house. I hated being alone in it all day, and then when he came home I got claustrophobic being with him all night, sharing the same bedroom, the same bath."

"Space is nice," I said.

"The feeling is still with me. It's why we don't live together."

"The way we live seems about right to me," I said.

"I know, but . . . when I married Brad, if people moved to twin beds you figured divorce was imminent."

"You didn't work."

"No. It would have embarrassed Brad to have his wife working. It would have implied he couldn't support her."

"Children?"

"Oh, God, yes. He wanted me to have children."

"And you didn't want to."

"Not then."

"Because?"

"I never knew. I just knew I couldn't."

"You know now?"

"It's something I've had a hard time thinking about," she said. "I must have sensed that this wasn't the right marriage to bring children into."

"Not so long ago you wanted us to have a kid."

"This isn't about me," Susan said.

"You think I'd try to rescue Brad from the feminists if you didn't ask me?"

"I know," Susan said. "But it's a part of my life I don't like to talk about."

"Like the part where you and I were separated?"

She was silent looking into her nearly full wine glass.

"If you had a patient," I said, "who couldn't talk about certain parts of her life, what would you tell her?"

Susan continued to look into her wine glass. Her shoulders looked stiff and angular. She didn't speak.

"I withdraw the question," I said.

She didn't look up from her wine glass.

"Thank you," she said. Her voice was tight.

"Got an address for Brad?" I said.

Silently she found a business card in her purse and took it out and handed it to me. The card read *Brad Sterling, Promotions*. Nice card. Good stock. Raised lettering. Not the kind of card you passed out if you were on the verge of dissolution. Unless you didn't want people to know you were on the verge of dissolution. Susan sat quietly while I looked at the card. Her shoulders hadn't eased much. She didn't look at me.

"You sure you want me to look into this?" I said.

"Absolutely," she said.

I nodded. This thing showed every sign of not working out well for me.

"I'll get right on it in the morning." I said.

two

TWO INSURANCE BUILDINGS tower over the Back Bay. The Hancock building is pretty good-looking if the windows don't fall out. The Prudential is ugly. Brad was in the Prudential. On the thirty-third floor. His receptionist looked like a J. Crew model, blonde Dutch boy haircut and slightly hollow cheeks.

"Do you have an appointment?" she asked.

She thought it unlikely but was being professional about it. The waiting room was empty.

"No," I said. "I don't."

She looked doubtful. Doubtful was a cute look for her.

"Well," she said, "I'm not sure . . ."

I gave her my card. The one that had my name and address but no reference to me being a sleuth.

"Tell him his ex-wife sent me."

Now she looked slightly embarrassed. Also a cute look. I suspected that she had practiced all of them in a mirror and discarded any that weren't cute.

"I, ah, there have been several . . ." she said.

"Susan," I said. "Susan Hirsch."

It was simple perversity that made me use her maiden name. The receptionist smiled appreciatively, as if I had told her an important thing. Her hand twitched as if she were going to pick up the phone but she didn't. Instead she said, "Excuse me," and stood and went into the inner office. She was there maybe five minutes and came out.

"Mr. Sterling has made room for you," she said.

"How nice," I said.

She gestured me into Sterling's office. It was a corner office with windows facing north and west so you could see the Charles River and Fenway Park and all the way to the horizon. Sterling stood as I came in and walked around his desk to meet me. He was a tall guy, leaner than I would have thought for a tackle, with a good tan. A good tan, in Boston, in March, means you've been south recently or want people to think so. His hair was longish and steel gray and went nicely with the tan. His gray pinstripe suit fit him well. He was wearing good cologne.

"Spenser, Brad Sterling," he said. "Nice to meet you."

His handshake was firm and genuine. He looked right at me as we shook. Then he motioned me toward one of the black captain's chairs in front of his desk. It had the Harvard seal on the back. On top of a file cabinet was a Harvard football helmet and framed on the wall was his varsity letter certificate.

"Pull up," Sterling said, "and sit."

I did. He went back around his desk and sat in his high-backed executive swivel and leaned back.

"Patti said something about Susan Hirsch," he said.

"Actually she still uses her married name," I said.

"Really. I'll be damned. I haven't seen Susan in years."

"Actually, you have," I said. "You saw her last week."

Sterling smiled.

"Except then," he said.

"And you told her you were in trouble, and you asked her for help."

"She told you that?"

"Uh huh."

He shook his head.

"Susan was always a little dramatic," he said.

"Yeah," I said. "Hysterical. Just because her ex-husband whom she hasn't seen in twenty years shows up asking for help . . ."

"Well, really, I didn't ask for help."

"Oh," I said. "Susan misunderstood. She thought you needed help and sent me over to provide it."

"What's your relation to Susan."

"Lover," I said.

Sterling widened his eyes and made a humorous snorting sound.

"Well, you are, by God, direct, aren't you?"

"Saves time," I said.

Sterling had his hands tented in front of him, the fingertips brushing his chin. He tapped his fingertips together a few times while he looked at me.

"Lesson there for me," he said. "That would make you the private eye."

"It would."

"I've heard about you. Always sort of amused me Susan would end up with . . . a private detective."

"Hard to figure," I said. "Want to tell me about your troubles?"

"So you can help me?"

"Yeah."

"Because Susan asked you to?"

"Yeah."

"How do you feel about helping out your girlfriend's ex?"

"She says I'll like you," I said.

He grinned. His teeth were very white and even.

"Of course you will," he said. "Everybody likes me."

"Susan says that you're being sued for sexual harassment."

"So, you're saying that somebody doesn't like me?"

"Tell me about it," I said.

He smiled and shrugged and leaned back farther in his chair and put his feet on the desk.

"I was running a thing at the Convention Center. Big charity do. Brought in Sister Sass from New York, had a ton of celebarooties. Message from the President. Lot of press."

"Which charity?"

"Sort of a fund-raiser gang-bang for all the deservings, you know? Care and placement of orphans, shelter for battered women, AIDS research, other intractable diseases, help for the homeless, safe streets programs, everybody in one swell foop."

"And?"

"And it was a blockbuster. I slept about two hours a night pulling it together, but it was a whizbang when we got it airborne."

"I sort of meant 'and the harassment'?"

"Oh, sure, of course."

Out the west window I could see the shadow of a cloud drift over Kenmore Square toward Fenway Park.

A little less than a month and baseball would be back. It seemed too early. It always did in March. Too cold to play ball, the ground too soggy. The wind too bold. But April always came and they played. I looked back at Sterling. He was sitting at his desk looking friendly.

"And the harassment?" I said.

"Nothing much, really," he said. "All these charities have a ton of volunteer do-gooders around. Mostly women, the kind who think they're important because their husbands are rich. And a lot of them are good-looking in that rich wife way, you know. Perfect hair-dos, expensive perfume, very silky. So I may have flirted with a couple of them, and they took it wrong."

"How would you define flirting?" I said.

I was almost sure that I opposed sexual harassment. I was less sure that I knew exactly what it was.

"You know, kidding around, telling them how good-looking they were. Hell I thought they'd be flattered. Most women are. Cripes, if they weren't married I'd figure them for a bunch of lesbos."

"Which is it, a 'couple,' or a 'bunch?' "

"There are four women participating in the lawsuit," Sterling said. "One of them is married to Francis Ronan."

"The law professor," I said.

"Him," Sterling said. "Talk about your luck running bad."

"You didn't touch these women?"

"Absolutely not," Sterling said.

"Were you obscene?"

"No, of course not."

"Did they work for you?"

"Not really. They were volunteers. I mean I was at

the top of the pyramid, I suppose, and they were down the slope a bit. But they didn't work for me."

"If you lose, can you pay the judgment?"

"That's not the point. I'm . . ." He grinned. "I'm an innocent man."

"But you could pay it."

"Certainly."

"You're not at the brink of, ah, dissolution?"

"Dissolute, yes, whenever possible," Sterling said. "Dissolution? Not hardly."

Sterling made a gesture that encompassed the office and the view. "This look like dissolution?"

"All it proves is they haven't evicted you," I said.

Sterling laughed out loud.

"A hard man is good to find," he said when he had stopped laughing.

"You want me to look into this a little?" I said. "See if I can fix it?"

"I wish someone would fix Francis Ronan," he said.

"Yes or no?"

"What do you charge?"

"Pro bono," I said.

"Well, the damn price is right, I guess. Sure, why not? You may as well take a whack at it."

"Okay. Who's your lawyer."

He shook his head.

"You don't have a lawyer?"

"Haven't got to it yet," he said. "Thought I'd wait until there was an actual court date. No point in paying some guy to shuffle papers for a month."

"Sometimes if a good lawyer shuffles them right, you don't have to go to court."

"Oh," he said, "a good lawyer."

And he leaned back in his chair and put his head

back and laughed again. It was a big laugh and sounded completely genuine.

"I'll need the names of the plaintiffs," I said.

"Sure. I had Patti start a file on this. Ask her for a copy."

I stood. He stood. We shook hands.

"Give Susan a kiss for me," he said.

"No," I said.

three

HAWK WAS SIPPING champagne at the corner of the bar in the Casablanca in Harvard Square and saving the bar stool next to him for me. As far as I could tell, no one had contested the seat.

"I ordered us a mess of pan-fried oysters," Hawk said. "Figured you could use the protein."

Jimmy the bartender looked at me and pointed to the Foster's tap. I nodded.

"Been here before?" Hawk said.

"Susan and I come here."

Jimmy brought the beer.

"Irish," Hawk said.

"His name is James Santo Costagnozzi," I said.

"Bad luck," Hawk said. "To look Irish when you not."

"Unless you're trying to pass," I said.

"Nobody trying to pass for Irish," Hawk said.

"Is that an ethnic slur?" I said.

"Believe so," Hawk said.

The pan-fried oysters arrived and we ate some.

"Feelin' stronger?" Hawk said.

"Potent is my middle name," I said.

"Always wondered," Hawk said. "How you doing with Susan's ex?"

"I met him today," I said.

"Umm," Hawk said.

"Umm?"

"Umm."

"What the hell does 'umm' mean?"

"Means how'd you feel talking with Susan's ex-husband."

"He seemed like kind of a goofball to me."

"Umm."

"His name was Silverman," I said. "He changed it to Sterling."

"Cute."

We ate some more oysters.

"He's got that sort of Ivy League old money WASP goofiness that they have," I said.

"Silverman?"

"Sterling," I said.

"So he trying to pass."

"I'd say so."

"And succeeding," Hawk said.

"Yes. He's got it down cold. Bow ties, everything."

"Maybe he just like bow ties."

"Who just likes bow ties?" I said.

"Got a point," Hawk said. "How he measure up?"

"To what?"

"To you."

"No better than anybody else."

Hawk grinned.

" 'Cept me," he said. "How you feel about him?"

"Something's wrong," I said. "Susan tells me he's at

the verge of dissolution. He says he's doing grand and has the office to prove it."

"So somebody lying," Hawk said.

"Right."

"And it ain't Susan."

"Also right."

"How she know he is in a state of near dissolution?" Hawk said.

"Wow," I said. "You talk like an Ivy Leaguer yourself."

"Ah's been practicin'," Hawk said. "How she know?"

"I assume he told her."

"So he either lying to her, or lying to you."

"And he hasn't got much reason to tell her he's going under if he's not," I said.

" 'Less he looking for sympathy."

"He's got no reason to," I said. "He's two, three wives past her."

"So why he go tell her his troubles?"

"Well, she's a good one if you need some help."

"How long since he seen her?"

I shrugged. "Maybe twenty years. She was already divorced when I met her."

"And now he decides she's a good listener?"

"Umm," I said.

"Tha's right," Hawk said.

We were quiet. Someone was playing The Platters on the jukebox. In the corner of the bar up high a hockey game played silently on television. The perfect compromise.

"Maybe knew about you," Hawk said.

"He wanted me he could walk into my office and tell me his problem," I said.

"And you'd do it free?"

I drank a little beer.

"You sound almost cynical," I said.

"Be the ghet-to experience," Hawk said, rolling the word ghetto into two long syllables. "Ah'm fighting to overcome it."

"So he knows about me and he needs help and he figures he can get it for nothing if he goes to Susan and cries dissolution."

"And it worked," Hawk said.

"If you're right," I said.

"Sure," Hawk said. "How you feel 'bout working for Susan's former husband?"

I shrugged. "Water over the dam," I said.

"Sure it is, and it really was the tooth fairy left all those quarters under your pillow."

"Got nothing to do with me," I said.

"That's true. But I know you, some of you, maybe not even Susan know. The hard part. Part makes you almost as good as me."

"Better," I said automatically.

"It ain't no water over no dam for that part," Hawk said.

I finished my beer. Jimmy brought me another pint.

" 'Course it's not," I said.

Hawk smiled. "Umm," he said.

"You got that right," I said.

"So you going to help him?"

"I told Susan I would."

"You think this sexual harassment suit be the problem?"

"Be surprised," I said. "But it's a place to start."

"Should we have some more oysters?" Hawk said.

"We'd be fools not to," I said.

four

MARCH WAS STILL chilly enough for a fire and I had one going in Susan's apartment when she came upstairs from her last appointment of the day. Pearl the Wonder Dog was lying on the rug in front of it, and I was on the couch with a bottle of my new favorite, Blue Moon Belgian White Ale, that Susan kept for me. It was not hard to locate. The only other thing in the refrigerator was a head of broccoli and two cans of Diet Coke.

Susan came in wearing her subdued professional wardrobe—dark suit, tailored blouse, understated makeup, little jewelry. When she was off duty she dressed far more flamboyantly. But she generated such intensity that dressing up or down made little difference.

Pearl got up at once, took a silk cushion from the wing chair, and carried it around wagging her tail. When Susan got that attended to, she got a bottle of Merlot out of the kitchen cabinet, poured half a glass, and brought it over to the couch. She plopped down beside me, put her feet up on the coffee table, leaned her head over, and kissed me lightly on the mouth.

"Some days are longer than others," she said.

Pearl eyed us speculatively, the pillow still in her mouth, and lay down by the fire and put her head on the pillow.

"Do you understand why she prances around with that pillow?" Susan said.

"No."

"Me either."

"Why was today so long?" I said.

Susan sighed and sipped her wine. It must have been a hell of a day, she took in nearly an ounce at one sip.

"One of the things a therapist runs into is the person who thinks now that they understand why they behave as they do, they are cured."

"And you think there may be another step?" I said.

"Changing the behavior would seem appropriate," Susan said.

"Appropriate," I said.

The logs settled a little in the fireplace. The front logs slid back in toward the back ones, making the fire more intense. I built a hell of a fire.

"The ability to understand doesn't automatically confer the ability to change."

"So people have another whole thing to go through," I said.

"Yep."

"And they don't like it."

"Nope," Susan said.

"And today you had several such people."

"Several."

We were quiet. She drank another swallow of wine and put her head against my shoulder.

"Been here long?" she said.

"No," I said. "I just got here. I had a couple beers with Hawk before I came."

"Pearl been fed?"

"Yep. Back yarded and fed."

"And a fire built," Susan said.

"I'd have started supper," I said, "but I didn't know whether you wanted your broccoli raw or simmered in Diet Coke."

"Umm," she said.

"Gee," I said, "Hawk often feels that way too."

We sat and looked into the fire and were quiet together. I liked it. It wasn't an absence of conversation; it was the presence of quiet.

"Saw your ex-husband this morning," I said.

Susan lifted her head from my shoulder and shifted slightly on the couch.

"Don't call him that," she said.

"Okay. I went to see the artist formerly known as Silverman today."

"And you don't have to be a smartass about it either," she said.

I nodded. This thing showed even more signs of not working out well for me.

"Shall I call him Brad?" I said.

"I really would rather not talk about him at all," Susan said.

"Even though you have employed me to save him."

"I didn't employ you," she said. "I asked for a favor."

It was something she did when she was angry, or

frightened, which made her angry; she focused vigorously on the wrong part of the question.

"That's right," I said, "you did."

In front of the fire Pearl got up quite suddenly and turned around three times and lay back down, this time with her back to the fire and her feet stretched out toward us. I wasn't aware that Susan had moved, exactly, but she was no longer in contact with me, and her shoulders were angular again.

"Want some more wine?" I said.

"No thank you."

We sat silently again. The silence crackled. It wasn't quiet now; it was anger. I got up and walked to the kitchen and looked out of Susan's window at the darkness.

"Suze," I said, "what the hell is going on?"

"Am I required to tell you everything about everybody I've ever known?"

"I don't recall asking you to do that," I said.

"Well, don't keep bringing up my marriage."

"Suze, for crissake, you came to me."

"I asked for your help, I didn't ask for your approval," she said.

She was a little nuts right now. She hadn't been until a moment ago. And she wouldn't be in a while. But right now there was no point talking.

"Okay," I said. "Here's the deal. I'll help Brad Sterling and I won't tell you about it unless you ask."

"Good."

"And now, I think I'll go home."

"Fine."

Pearl followed me with her eyes as I walked from the kitchen, and her tail wagged slowly, but she didn't lift her head. I reached down and patted her and went to the front door.

"Good night," I said.

"Good night."

I stopped on my way home to pick up some Chinese food and when I got to my place the message light on my machine was flashing. I put the food, still in cartons, in the oven on low and went and played the message.

Susan's voice said, "I'm sorry. Please call me tomorrow."

I poured a little Irish whisky in a glass with a couple of ice cubes. Scotch and beer were recreational, and now and then a martini. Irish whisky was therapeutic. I stood at my front window and drank the whisky. The apartment was very silent. Outside there was a wind, which was unusual—normally the wind died down at night—and it blew a couple of Styrofoam cups around on Marlborough Street. The argument made me feel lousy, but I'd get over it and so would she—the connection between us was too strong to break. What bothered me more was that I couldn't figure out what caused us to argue. Below me, a woman in a long coat was walking a yellow Lab toward Arlington Street. The dog, eager on his leash, had his head down into the wind. But his tail was moving happily and he sniffed at everything. I took a little whisky. In Susan's anger there was something else besides anger. Under the brisk annoyance was a soundless harmonic that I hadn't heard in a long time. She wasn't afraid of much. And when she was afraid it made her furious. The dog paused at Arlington Street and then crossed when the light changed without any sign that I could see from the woman holding the leash. Some-

thing about Brad Sterling scared her. It wouldn't be
Brad as Brad. The only thing Susan was ever really
scared of was herself. It would have to be something
that Brad stood for. If it were someone else, I could ask
her about it. But it was her. The dog was out of sight
now, in the dark of the Public Garden, probably off
leash at this time of night, rushing about tracking rats
along the edges of the swan boat pond, having a hell of
a time. I drank some more whisky. This thing showed
every sign of not working out well for me.

five

If THERE WERE four women suing somebody and one of them was married to Francis Ronan, she figured to be the point person in the deal. So I went to see her first.

Jeanette Ronan lived with her husband in an important, old, vast, gray-shingled house on the outer side of Marblehead Neck, with the Atlantic Ocean washing up over the brassy rock outcroppings at the bottom of their backyard. There was a low fieldstone fence across the front of the property with short fieldstone pillars on each side of the entrance. The property was hilly and scattered with old trees, still unleaved in late winter. The driveway, which curved up to the right and out of sight behind the house, was covered with red stone dust, and there were a lot of flower beds, inert in the loveless March sunlight. I parked at the top of the hill in a big turn-around, beside a red Mercedes sport coupe and a silver Lexus sedan. There was enough room left over to park a couple of tour buses and a caviar truck.

The house had a wide veranda that wrapped around

three sides. I walked up the low steps from the drive-way and rang. Through the double glass doors I could see a central hallway, with Persian scatter rugs on the polished oak floor, and bright brass fixtures on the walls. Didn't look like faculty housing to me. A woman with a lot of blonde hair and a good tan walked down the hallway and opened the door. She was very nice looking. I handed her my card.

"Mrs. Ronan?"

"Yes, you're Mr. Spenser."

I agreed that I was and we went in.

"My husband is in the conservatory," she said.

I had made the appointment with her, but I didn't comment. We walked the length of the hallway, which gave me a chance to examine her hip movement in case I ever had to follow her covertly. I wondered if that were sexual harassment. Is there sexual harass-ment if the victim doesn't know it? If a tree falls in the forest . . . We turned right at the end of the hallway and went into a glass room. The room overlooked the At-lantic, thirty feet below, and the spray from some of the waves breaking on the rocks spattered onto the glass. The effect was pretty good.

Francis Ronan was having coffee. He put his cup down on the mahogany coffee table and got up from his brown leather arm chair. A copy of the *New York Times* lay open on the floor beside the chair.

"Mr. Spenser," Jeanette said, "my husband, Francis Ronan."

Ronan was obviously older than his wife, but not much bigger. I put out my hand. Ronan didn't really shake hands. He simply handed you his and allowed you to squeeze it for a moment. He was a thin guy with a bald head and a deep tan. I was running into a lot of tans lately. I tried not to look pallid.

"Coffee?" Ronan said.

"That would be nice," I said.

"Jeanette," Ronan said, and his wife stepped around to the coffee table and poured some coffee from a silver pitcher into a white bone china cup.

"Cream and sugar?"

I said yes and she put some of each into the cup and handed it to me. Apparently I was expected to drink it myself. Ronan nodded at another brown leather chair across from him, and I sat. Jeanette Ronan took a chair to her husband's left. Unless she had a special deal with God, she obviously worked out a lot. And effectively. Ronan studied me over his coffee cup for a time. He wore glasses and it made his eyes seem bigger than they were, though it would have been hard for them to be smaller. I think I was supposed to shift uneasily in my chair under Ronan's gaze, but I had been gazed at by a lot of people, and I was able to remain calm. I drank some coffee. It was good coffee. Ronan would have good coffee. Below us I could hear the surf. It sounded just right. Ronan would have quality surf. And fine cigars. And a grand home. And the best brandy. And a slick-looking wife. And some dandy white bone china cups to stare over. Finally he took a sip and put the cup down.

"Well," Ronan said. "Go ahead."

"I was hoping to talk with Mrs. Ronan about her sexual harassment suit against Brad Sterling," I said.

"Go ahead."

"Tell me about the sexual harassment," I said.

She smiled courteously and looked at her husband.

"Mrs. Ronan would prefer not to go over that again," Ronan said.

"Did he touch you?" I said.

"You are impertinent, sir," Ronan said.

"That's widely acknowledged," I said.

"It is not a quality I admire."

"What can you tell me about your relationship with Brad Sterling?" I said to Jeanette.

She shook her head before the question was even finished.

"I had no . . ."

"I am afraid this interview is over," Ronan said.

"Hard to tell," I said.

"Jeanette, perhaps you can excuse yourself," Ronan said.

She smiled and nodded. She stood. I stood. Ronan remained seated. She put out her hand. I took it. It was much firmer and warmer than her husband's.

"Nice to have met you, Mr. Spenser," she said.

"You're just saying that."

Her smile remained polite as she left the glass room. I looked at Ronan. He had poured himself a little more coffee from his silver coffee carafe into his white bone china cup, and was adding a single cube of sugar with a small pair of silver tongs.

"You had no intention of telling me anything," I said. "Why did you agree to see me?"

Ronan made a thin lip movement that he probably thought was a smile.

"I like to get the measure of people," he said.

"And you think you can do it in this amount of time?"

"I believe I can," he said. "And I want them to get the measure of me."

"Sure," I said. "About five foot six. Right?"

"I have no interest in jokes, Spenser. Nor, frankly, any further interest in you. I have learned what I need to know. Granted, you are physically imposing. You would probably make a good bouncer. But in any way that matters, you are a lightweight. I can reach into every crevice of this state. Should you become an irritant, I can have you squished like an insect. You are way out of your league here, and it would be in your best interest to recognize that."

"Squished?" I said.

Ronan didn't answer. He seemed entirely satisfied with his assessment of me and had nothing to add.

"You college professors are a tough bunch," I said.

Ronan smiled almost indulgently.

"I am at the moment associated with a university," he said. "But surely you know my career."

"Not as well as I will."

Ronan laughed out loud.

"Well, really?" he said. "Was that a threat?"

"I guess so," I said. "You are, after all, an annoying little twerp."

I thought Ronan might have colored a little under his tan, but his voice revealed nothing. He stood.

"As I said, you would make a good bouncer. Let me show you the way out."

Driving back across the causeway toward the rest of Marblehead, I wondered what there was in a simple harassment suit to make Ronan lean on me so hard.

Six

I WAS WITH Susan. We were lying in bed at my apartment with my arm under her shoulders and her head on my chest. Pearl was in exile somewhere outside the bedroom door.

"One of us should probably get up and let the baby in," Susan said.

"Absolutely," I said.

We lay still.

"Well?" Susan said.

"I thought you were volunteering," I said.

"You're closest to the door."

"True," I said.

"And you're a guy," she said.

"That clinches it," I said.

I got up and opened the bedroom door. Pearl bounded into the room, gave me a sidelong look which might have been reproachful, and hopped up on the bed in my spot.

"This didn't work out exactly as I'd hoped," I said.

"She'll move," Susan said, and, in fact Pearl did. She moved huffily down to the foot of the bed and turned around three or four times and lay down. I put my arm back under Susan's shoulders. She put her head back on my chest. Pearl put her head on my right shinbone.

"My mother would never allow the dog anywhere but outside or in the kitchen," Susan said.

"Barbaric."

"I think that was a more general rule in those days," she said.

"How long have we been together?" I said.

"Roughly since the beginning of time," she said.

"Or longer," I said. "And I barely know where you grew up."

"Never seemed to matter."

"No," I said. "It didn't. I guess we kind of liked the sense of living in the immediate present."

"It was a way to symbolize that what happened before we met didn't matter."

"Yes," I said.

Outside my bedroom window, in the oblique bluish glare of the street lamps, I could see snow falling. It was falling lightly, a spring snow, the flakes spaced wide apart. It was the best kind of snow, because this far into March you knew it wouldn't last. Baseball season opened in nineteen days.

"So, you grew up in Swampscott," I said.

"Now it matters?" Susan said.

"It matters to you," I said.

She was quiet. With her forefinger she traced on my chest the outline of a bullet wound that I'd survived.

"I guess everyone has scars," Susan said. "Yours, at least, show."

"I got shot in the ass once in London," I said.

"I always suspected you were mooning the shooter," she said.

Outside the window the snowflakes were smaller, and coming faster, and straight down. Susan stopped tracing the scar on my chest and put her hand down flat over it.

"So, I grew up in Swampscott," Susan said.

"I knew that."

"My father was a pharmacist. Hirsch Drug on Humphrey Street. My mother was a housewife."

"No sisters or brothers," I said.

"They were childless until me. My father was forty-one when I was born. My mother was thirty-eight."

"How'd that happen?" I said.

"I don't think it was intentional," Susan said. "My mother never talked much about that kind of thing. Actually, my mother probably didn't know too much about that kind of thing."

"Being born late could work either way for you," I said.

She laughed, though I didn't hear humor in it.

"Actually it went both ways. My father was ecstatic. My mother was not."

"Feeling displaced?"

"I'm afraid so."

"Easy thing to feel," I said. "If she'd been the sole object of your father's affection for what, ten, fifteen years?"

"Eighteen."

"Then she is suddenly faced with competition at the precise moment when she is least able to compete."

"Because she's tired most of the time," Susan said. "Stuck home with the baby, and Papa comes home after a pleasant day at the drug store, plays with the baby for an hour and says 'ain't it great.' "

"And your mother feels like there's something unwomanly about her because she doesn't think it's so great."

"In fact, she resents the baby," Susan said.

"Which makes her feel worse, which makes her resent the baby more."

"My God," Susan said, "I'm naked in bed with a sensitive male."

"Man of the nineties," I said.

"No matter how often," Susan said, "it is always surprising that you know the things you know."

"You hang around," I said, "you learn."

"Depends on who you hang around with," Susan said.

"I spend a lot of my life with people in trouble," I said. "I think some of them would have been in trouble if they'd been brought up by Mother Teresa, but a lot of them come from homes where the family didn't work right for them."

"We meet the same kinds of people, don't we."

"Except the kind you meet have managed to get themselves to a shrink."

"Unless they are a shrink," Susan said.

"Then they give themselves a referral," I said.

We were quiet. Enough snow had collected on Marlborough Street to reflect the street lights, and the darkness outside my bedroom window had become somewhat paler. Susan still had her hand flat over the pale scars on my chest.

Susan said, "We're skating very carefully on the surface here, aren't we."

"Yes."

"That's because we're on very thin ice."

"I know."

"It's not like you to be so oblique," she said.

"It's not like us to be on thin ice," I said.

"I . . . I'll get past this," Susan said.

"I know."

"But you'll have to bear with me," she said. "Right now this is the best I can do."

"I'll bear with you," I said, "until hell freezes over."

"There would be some really thin ice," Susan said.

She took her hand off my scars and put it against my face and raised up and kissed me hard. Hell could freeze solid if it wanted to.

Seven

I PICKED RITA Fiore up at Cone, Oakes and Baldwin, where she was their senior litigator, and took her to lunch at the Ritz Cafe. The maitre d' got her a table by the window and let me sit there too.

"Is this a three-martini lunch?" Rita said.

"If you can control yourself," I said.

"I have always controlled myself," Rita said. "Except maybe with that Assistant DA when I was in Norfolk County."

We each ordered a martini. I had one made with vodka, on the rocks, with a twist. Rita was a classicist. She had it straight up with gin and olives. Outside our window on Newbury Street the snow that had fallen last night had melted except in corners where there was always shade. Rita drank her first drink and held it in her mouth for a minute and closed her eyes. Then she swallowed.

"Good," Rita said. "What do you need?"

"Maybe I've missed you," I said.

"Yeah, and maybe you're going to guzzle down two martinis and come on to me."

"In the Ritz Cafe?" I said.

"Of course not," Rita said. "So what do you want?"

"Francis Ronan," I said.

Rita paused with her glass halfway to her lips. She leaned back in her chair and looked at me.

"You're not going to law school."

"No."

She kept looking at me. Then, as if she finally realized that she was holding it, she raised her martini glass and took another swallow and put the glass down.

"Working for or against?" she said.

"Probably against," I said.

"That figures," Rita said.

"Why does that figure?" I said.

"Sir Lancelot asks you about a dragon, you don't figure they're working together."

"I'm Sir Lancelot?"

"You think you are."

"Which makes Francis Ronan a dragon."

"Not so loud," Rita said.

"He has people everywhere?" I said.

"He knows a lot of people and some of them are the kind that have lunch here."

"Like us," I said.

"No," Rita said. "Not like us."

"So, tell me about him?"

"First, none of this is for attribution," Rita said.

She had lowered her voice, though I don't think she realized it.

"What am I, *Newsweek*?" I said.

"I mean it. You'll have to promise me that you will not tell anyone that I talked to you about Francis Ronan."

"You sound scared, Rita."

"I am."

"I didn't think you were scared of anything."

"I'm scared of him," Rita said. "You should be too."

"Me? Sir Lancelot?"

"You promise or no?" Rita said.

"I promise."

"Okay. I'll tell you everything I know about him. But first some free advice."

"Free?" I said. "You sure you're a lawyer?"

"Stay away from Francis Ronan. You have a case that brings you into conflict with him, get off the case."

"Thank you," I said.

"For what?"

"For the advice."

"You going to take it?"

"No."

"I didn't imagine you would," she said. "But it was serious advice. What do you want to know."

"Everything you can tell me," I said.

Rita leaned forward and spoke so softly that I had to lean forward too.

"He is a legendary lawyer," Rita said. "You know that. He is the finest criminal defense lawyer I have ever seen. He's so smart, he's so . . . what is he . . . he's so . . . he wants so badly to win that he commits everything to every defense. Nothing else matters to him as much as getting his client acquitted. He will do anything to win. And he's that way regardless of the merit of his client's case, or, for that matter, the merit of the client."

"He's represented some very bad people," I said.

"The worst, and he's won for them. And the best, and he's won for them."

"And it's made him rich."

Rita finished her martini and ordered another one. I was still dawdling with mine. Martinis make me sleepy. Consumed at lunch they tend to blow my day, as is true at breakfast.

"Yes. Actually, I think he was always rich. I think his family had money. But he has certainly enlarged his net worth over the years."

"And he was a judge," I said.

"Yes. Interestingly, he was not a terribly good judge. He is not judicious. He is not a great legal mind. He is a great litigator. But his judicial rulings were frequently reversed on appeal. He hadn't the patience, or, I guess, the sense of fairness of"—again Rita looked for a word—"of decency," she said, "that makes a good judge."

"How'd he feel about being overruled?"

"It is said to have driven him mad," Rita said. "Have you met him?"

"Yes."

"Has he an ego?"

"A lot bigger than he is," I said.

"It's what made him so good as a litigator. The ego. He needed to win."

Rita had picked up the menu and looked at it as she talked. Now she paused to read it.

"Lobster sandwich looks good," she said.

"You going to have it?" I said.

"Oh, God no," she said. "With these hips, what are you crazy?"

"Those are elegant hips," I said.

Rita snorted and put down the menu.

"I'll have the green salad," she told the waiter, "dressing on the side."

I ordered the lobster sandwich.

"You're doing that to be mean," Rita said.

"I like lobster sandwiches. What's Ronan doing at Taft?"

"Ego. He may be the greatest criminal lawyer in the world. But criminal lawyers tend to represent criminals. And some of the dirt maybe rubs off. I think he took the professorship at Taft because it was prestigious."

"Does he actually teach," I said.

Rita shrugged.

"Taft's trying to build the law school. One way to do that is to attract a superstar. As you know, one of the prime perks of any teaching job is not to teach. Ronan is a superstar. My guess is that he probably lectures once a week. I think he would enjoy lecturing."

"How about the wife?"

"Don't know much about her. She's not his first wife. She's a lot younger, and the couple of times I've seen her she was a knockout."

"So why is he so dangerous?" I said.

"Because in any adversarial circumstance he will do anything to win. He is very wealthy and he is hugely connected, including all the bad guys he's defended."

The waiter came with Rita's salad and my lobster sandwich, with mayo, on sourdough bread. Rita ate some salad. I had a bite of my lobster sandwich.

"Pig," she said.

I nodded modestly.

"So how come you are involved with Ronan?" Rita said.

"His wife and three other women are suing Susan's ex-husband for sexual harassment."

"Susan's ex-husband?"

"Yes. Guy named Brad Sterling. He changed it from Silverman."

"Yeah. Swell. I was thinking of changing mine to Fire."

"Fire Fiore?" I said.

"No, idiot, Rita Fire, attorney-at-law. So what's your deal with Sterling Silverman?"

"Susan asked me to see if I could help him out. She says he's on the brink of dissolution."

Rita stared at me. "Susan asked you to save her ex-husband?"

"In a manner of speaking."

"And you're doing it?"

"I'm looking into it."

"And you have to go against Francis Ronan to do it?"

"Maybe."

Rita stared at me some more. "Are you out of your fucking mind?" Rita said.

"Not yet."

Rita started to speak and stopped and started again and stopped without saying anything. She sat silently shaking her head.

"You told Hawk about this yet?" she said finally.

"Yeah."

"He have any comment?"

"He said, 'Umm.'"

"You got any idea what he meant by that?"

"I think he was implying that this enterprise is fraught with peril."

"Umm," Rita said.

"Maybe," I said.

"You say you've met Ronan?"

"Yeah."

Rita smiled. "And did you get along?"

"Not really well," I said.

She smiled wider. "Were you properly respectful?"

"I told him he was an annoying little twerp," I said.

Rita laughed out loud, and a couple of people in tweed clothing looked up from their scrod and stared at her. Rita met their look and held it, and they looked quickly back at their scrod.

"I don't mean to laugh," Rita said. "It is actually quite serious, but goddamn! You and Francis Ronan." She shook her head still smiling. "A match made in heaven," she said. "You're as arrogant as he is."

"And taller," I said.

"Be careful with him," Rita said. "Be carefuller than you have ever been with anybody."

"Sure," I said. "And maybe he needs to be careful of me."

Rita looked at her glass, discovered a little undrunk martini in the bottom. She picked it up and drained it and put the glass down carefully in the exact same spot where she had picked it up.

"Maybe," she said.

eight

ACCORDING TO THE list Sterling's secretary had given me, there were three other women in the harassment suit: Olivia Hanson, Marcia Albright, and Penny Putnam. Penny Putnam lived in an apartment on the water where the Charlestown Navy Yard used to be. I decided to visit her first. It was close and I like alliteration.

Penny's address was a big rambling gray clapboard white-trim apartment complex on Pier 7. There was parking under, and the front door was a flight up. A big pretty woman answered the door. I asked if she were Penny Putnam, and she said that she was. She smiled. She was friendly. I could tell she liked me. I asked if I could ask a few questions about the sexual harassment suit she was involved in, and the valves of her attention closed like a stone.

"I'm sorry," she said. "I have no comment."

"Why not?" I said.

The door closed more firmly than the valves of her attention. So the trip shouldn't be a complete waste of time, I stood for a moment and looked across the harbor at the downtown waterfront. Nice view. Then I turned and went back to my car and drove away. I was still sure she liked me. Her rejection was circumstantial. I went across the Charlestown Bridge and picked up the Central Artery near North Station. They had built a third tunnel under the Harbor and were in the process of dismantling the Central Artery and putting it underground. The result was that City Square had disappeared and there were convoluted detours from Charlestown to Mattapan. It was always exciting to see where you would end up.

Marcia Albright lived in Quincy, and Olivia Hanson lived in Malden. I figured I'd get the Southeast Expressway over with, so I headed for Quincy. Marcia's place was very much like Penny's—an apartment complex with a water view, only Marcia's was brick. I never did find out what Marcia looked like. I got as far as the intercom and was told that she had no comment and the line went dead. Only because I'm methodical, I went back up the expressway, over the Mystic River Bridge, and a short haul up Route 1 to another apartment complex. This one, in Malden, designed to look like, I guess, a Moorish castle. If you got in just the right place, there was a view of the Saugus River.

Olivia Hanson was much nicer than Penny or Marcia. She actually came out into the vestibule and spoke with me.

"Oh, no," she said. "I'm terribly sorry. But I really couldn't comment on the lawsuit."

"On advice of counsel?" I said.

"Whatever," she said and gave me a lovely smile. She was smallish and perky and had a lot of blonde hair. "Are you a lawyer?"

"No," I said. "I'm a detective."

"Really? Can I see a badge or something?"

I showed her my license.

"Wow," she said. "You're a private detective. Do you have a gun?"

"Yes," I said. "But it's kind of small."

She widened her eyes at me. "Is that like an off-color remark?" she said.

I opened my jacket and let her see the short-barreled Smith & Wesson .38 I was wearing.

"Oh it is small, isn't it?" she said.

I grinned.

"But sufficient," I said. "Did Brad Sterling make some off-color remarks?"

"Don't try and trick me," she said. "I told you I'm not supposed to talk about that with anyone."

"Who says?"

She smiled at me and shook her head. "No, no, no," she said.

We did about five more minutes of that in the vestibule until even my killer charm was beginning to wear thin. I looked at my watch. Maybe bribery.

"Care for some lunch?" I said.

She shook her head again. My killer charm was apparently threadbare.

"No, I don't think I better."

"My loss," I said, ever gallant.

"But maybe sometime, once the legal stuff is over," she said. "I'll take a rain check."

I wrote "lunch—rain check" on the back of one of my business cards and handed it to her. We shook hands and I left the vestibule and got in my car and went back to Boston.

nine

For dinner at Chez Henri, Susan was wearing a gray top with gray pants and a wide black belt. It was one of my favorite outfits. Chez Henri was in Cambridge, just off Mass Ave, a nice informal room, open and high ceilinged, with a plate-glass window across the front that looked out on Shepard Street. I suppose it would be less egocentric to remark that it also looked in on the restaurant from Shepard Street. But from my perspective, it looked out. And I had no real wish to avoid egocentricity. I was eating baked oysters with some spinach on them. Susan had chicken and mashed potatoes. I was helping her with the mashed potatoes.

"You remember the first time you ate out?" I said.

"Sure," she said. "And you?"

"Yeah, some diner outside Laramie, I think. One of my uncles took me. I had a ham and egg sandwich."

She smiled. "My father used to take us to dinner every Friday night at the dining room of the Hotel Edison in Lynn."

"Lynn?"

"Before the shoe factories moved out. The Edison was still quite fancy."

"What did you have?"

"Lobster pie." Susan smiled at the memory. "Lobster out of the shell, covered with bread crumbs soaked with melted butter, and baked. If someone served that to me now, I would probably feel faint."

"But then?" I said.

Susan was drinking Merlot with her chicken, daring to be different. She looked into her glass for a moment and sipped a small amount.

"I loved it. Who knew about good for you?" She smiled again. It was the smile which hinted of fun and something slightly evil. "And it drove my mother crazy."

"Lobster pie?"

"No, me. I know she wanted to get a sitter and leave me home."

"They ever do that?"

"No," Susan said. I could hear the echo of childhood triumph even now. "I went almost everywhere with him."

"Way to go," I said.

She laughed.

"Do I still sound that triumphant?" she said.

"Yes."

"One never entirely outgrows one's childhood," she said.

"You going to eat those mashed potatoes," I said.

"Just leave me this much."

She marked off a section with the tines of her fork.

"So your mother was jealous of you," I said.

"Yes, I'm sure she was. My father was her link to

the world. She didn't drive. She rarely went anywhere, except with him. She was aaaalways home."

"And now she had to share him."

Susan smiled again. "Unequally," she said.

ten

I WAS SITTING IN my office thinking about Susan. I had left the door ajar to encourage impulse buyers, and to keep an eye on Lila the receptionist in the interior design showroom across the hall. I had no carnal interest in Lila, but I liked to keep track of her costumes. Today she was wearing a white turtleneck and farmer overalls and high-heeled sneakers. She had stopped spiking her hair a while ago, though she had kept the metallic streaks, and it now lay waveless and long, below her shoulders.

My view of Lila was obliterated by a tall fat man who came through the open door of my office followed by a short thick man with a small head. The fat man was wearing a shiny leather jacket, necessarily unzipped, with a white shirt under. The collar points of his shirt were carefully folded out over the jacket collar. He was clean shaven and his black hair was slicked back. He had a freshly washed pink moist look to his face, like he'd just come from a steam bath. The short guy was very thick. His neck was wider than his head, and his lats were so swollen that his arms made an A line out from his body. He had on a white dress shirt buttoned to the neck.

"You Spenser?" the fat man said.

His voice was raspy and high.

"Yes I am," I said.

The fat man closed the door behind him and the short thick guy leaned on it with his arms folded. Don't they all.

"We got a business arrangement to discuss with you," the fat man said.

I nodded toward one of my client chairs. The fat man ignored me. Probably wouldn't have fit in it anyway.

"You're working on a thing," the fat man said. "And we want you to stop."

"Which thing you have in mind?" I said.

"Thing with ah, Sterling, thing about the sexual harassing."

"You want me to stop looking into that?"

"Yeah."

"What's in it for me?"

"I been authorized to pay you for your time," the fat man said. He pronounced it *autorized*. "And also, like, a bonus."

"Sort of an outplacement package," I said.

"Whatever," the fat man said.

"How much you authorized to pay?" I said.

"A week's work at your standard rate, and a grand bonus."

"Who do you represent?" I said.

"I ain't authorized to tell you that."

"And what if I decline?"

"Huh?"

"What if I tell you to buzz off?"

"You get a bad beating."

I nodded thoughtfully. "Buzz off," I said.

The fat guy looked startled. His buddy with the undersized head didn't look anything.

"You think we're fooling around?"

"I think you can't pull it off," I said.

"The two of us against you?" the fat guy said.

"Doesn't seem fair," I said, "does it. Maybe if I kept one hand in my pocket."

"Fun-ny," the fat man said. "Is he a funny guy, Bullet?"

Bullet didn't comment on whether I was funny or not.

"Last chance," the fat man said. "Take the deal or the beating."

I stood up behind my desk.

"Buzz off," I said.

"Bullet," the fat man said.

Bullet left the door and walked toward me. He seemed to be walking on the balls of his feet. He moved lightly for a guy as wide as he was. As he came around the desk after me, I moved to my left, keeping the desk between us. The fat man stood back a little. Probably didn't want my blood splattering all over his white shirt. Now Bullet was behind my desk and I was in front of it. The fat man took another half step back to stay out of the way. He was amused at the ring around that I was playing with Bullet. I did a sharp half turn with my upper body and hit the fat man with my elbow on his right cheek and turned back toward Bullet who came in a rush angling to cut me off before I got the desk between us again, but I didn't try to get the desk between us. I kicked him in the groin instead and turned back toward the fat man and hit him a left, right combination and the fat man went back against the wall and slid slowly down it to slump on the floor with his legs splayed out in front of him as I spun back again to Bullet. He was down, so I took my gun off my hip and went and sat on the edge of my desk. The fat guy was sitting against the wall beside the door staring at nothing, waiting for his head to clear. There was a red mouse under his right eye that would darken and enlarge over the next few days. Bullet lay silently on his side. I knew what he was doing. He was waiting for the waves of crampy pain to stop. But he showed no sign that he was in pain. He showed no sign of anything. He simply lay motionless on his side with his knees bent. I sat on the edge of my desk and held my gun without pointing it and waited and didn't say anything.

"Okay," the fat man said after a while. "Okay."

I nodded helpfully.

"You sucker punched me," he said.

His right eye was beginning to narrow as the mouse under it continued to expand.

"Yes," I said. "I did."

He nodded his head slowly. His eyes were still dull as he looked at me. "Okay," he said. "So you get the beating another day."

"I like optimism," I said.

"Oh, you'll get it," the fat guy said. "Bullet and me maybe misjudged you a little. Nobody told us you'd be a hard case. But next time we'll know that, won't we, Bullet?"

Bullet had recovered enough to sit up with his back to me. He didn't say anything. The fat guy nodded as if Bullet had answered.

"Yeah. We'll come at it a little different," he said. "Next time."

"Might want to bring more people," I said. "Even the odds up a little."

"We can bring more people, we need to," the fat man said. "We got some people we could bring, huh, Bullet?"

Bullet got himself slowly onto his feet and walked flatfooted now, and much less lightly over to the fat man and put down a hand and pulled the fat man to his feet.

"You've bought yourself a lotta trouble, pal," the fat man said.

"All part of the service," I said.

"You sure you don't want to think about this," the fat guy said. "A week's pay plus a grand?"

"Buzz off," I said.

Again the fat man shrugged.

"Okay by me," he said. "Bullet 'n me would just as soon beat the crap out of you anyway. Which we will do at another time. Right, Bullet?"

Bullet stood silently holding the door. His eyes were very small and they were very close to his nose.

"See you around," the fat man said and walked out.

Bullet followed him. Neither of them was moving very briskly. Their footsteps receded and paused. I heard the elevator. I heard the elevator doors open and shut. I got up and walked to the door and checked the corridor. They had, in fact, buzzed off.

I walked back to my desk and put the Smith & Wesson on my blotter and sat down with my feet up and thought about their offer.

eleven

HENRY CIMOLI'S HARBOR Health Club had continued its upscale climb. The number of big old York barbells had dwindled and the number of shiny weight-lifting machines had increased. Hawk and I, always flexible, were adjusting well, though both of us still did curls the old-fashioned way. We were there together on a bright morning when it was still too cold to really be spring. Through the picture windows across the back, the harbor looked bleak and choppy, and the sea birds looked cold. Hawk was resting between sets on the lat machine, watching Henry Cimoli taking a client through what must have been the first workout of his life.

Clients loved Henry. They figured if they paid attention, they could look like he did. And they were right, if they happened to have his genes. Henry had been a lightweight boxer with the scar tissue around his eyes to prove it. His weight was the same as it had been when he fought. He wore a white tee shirt and white satin warm-up pants, and he looked like a pint and a half of muscle stuffed into a pint shirt.

The new client was doing a bench press with no weight on the machine. He was wearing a leopard-print sweatband, black fingerless weight-lifting gloves, a black tanktop, black shorts, and high-top black basketball shoes with no socks. His legs were pale and skinny. His arms were pale and skinny. He had a tattoo on each shoulder.

"Excellent," Henry said. "Now, let's try it this time with the pin in."

"My wife doesn't want me to get overdeveloped," the guy said.

"Sure," Henry said. "We'll be real careful about that. How's this weight?"

The guy did a big exhale and pushed up one plate of the weight stack.

"Terrific," Henry said. "Ter-rif-ic. Now let's go for ten."

The client cranked out eight and stopped.

"Dynamite," Henry said. "You'll be doing ten in no time."

The guy was breathing too hard to answer. When he sat up on the bench he showed a surprising belly for a skinny guy. Hawk stopped watching and did another set on the machine, his face expressionless, his movements almost serpentine as the muscles swelled and subsided with each repetition. Henry moved his client to the next room to do leg presses. He kept a perfectly straight face as he walked past Hawk and me. Hawk finished his second set and got up and got a drink of water and came back.

"Fat guy," he said thoughtfully, "and a fireplug named Bullet. Must be new in town, or new in the business."

I nodded. It was an unusual local thug that neither of us knew.

"Be coming back though," Hawk said. "Sluggers don't much like getting their ass kicked by the designated sluggee."

"I'd sort of like to know who sent them," I said.

"You guessing Ronan?"

"Rita says he's got the connections," I said, "And the temperament."

"Makes you wonder how good his wife's case is on the sexual harassment," Hawk said. "He trying to chase you off the case."

He settled onto the bench, set the pin at 250 pounds, and began doing chest presses.

"Yeah, but is he going to court with a case that can't stand investigation?" I said.

"Nobody will talk to you about it," Hawk said.

The weight bar moved smoothly up and down as he talked. His voice remained normal. His breathing was even.

"Well, it makes sense that the women won't talk," I said. "Any lawyer would tell them to shut up and save it for court."

"Hell," Hawk said. "Your own client ain't telling you doo dah."

"Doo dah?"

"Doo dah."

Hawk continued to push the bar up and let it down.

"How many reps so far?"

"Twenty-eight," Hawk said. "Why you suppose your client ain't telling you doo dah?"

"While I haven't phrased it to myself so gracefully," I said, "I have been considering that question."

"And what have you come up with?"

"Doo dah," I said.

"So maybe he don't want you in it," Hawk said.

"Wasn't our previous theory that he did, which was why he brought his problem to Susan?"

"Uh huh."

Hawk drove the bar up a final time and let it down.

"So how many reps is that," I said.

"Forty-two," he said.

"You were either aiming for forty and decided to do a couple extra," I said, "or you were hoping for forty-five and couldn't make it."

Hawk sat up from the bench and smiled. There was a glisten of sweat on his smooth head.

"Maybe you wrong in your previous theory," he said.

"Actually, I believe it was your theory."

"A foolish consistency," Hawk said, "be the hobgoblin of little minds."

"Of course it be," I said. "So if he doesn't want me in it, why doesn't he say so?"

"Don't know," Hawk said.

"Well, why did he go to Susan with it?"

"Maybe he just need to whine a little," Hawk said, "and Susan, being Susan, take the whining seriously, and take action and now Sterling don't know how to get out of it without looking foolish."

"So maybe he sent the sluggers," I said.

"You the detective," Hawk said.

"How can you tell?" I said.

"Mostly guesswork," Hawk said. "Why don't we take some steam while we here and got Henry to protect us, then I'll trail along with you, case the sluggers show up with, ah, tactical support."

"I'll just tell them you did forty-two reps with two hundred fifty and they'll surrender without a struggle."

"Or I could shoot them," Hawk said.

"That would be effective," I said.

On our way to the steam room we passed Henry who was working with a new client.

"No ma'am," he was saying. "Most women don't bulk up from exercise."

twelve

"JUST WHAT DID you do to these women?" I said to Brad Sterling, "that caused them to bring suit against you?"

We were at an outdoor cafe on Newbury Street. I was drinking beer. Sterling had a glass of Chartreuse. It was sixty degrees with no wind. Almost April. Spring. Yippee.

"Nothing," Sterling said. "That's the damned shame of it. I didn't do anything. The case is ridiculous."

"You are being charged with sexual harassment by the wife of the most prominent trial lawyer in the country," I said. "Whether you did anything or not, the case is not ridiculous."

"Oh hell," he said. "I may have kidded them a little. They liked it. You see a lovely girl, what can be the harm, letting her know she's lovely?"

"Do you have a lawyer yet?" I said.

"No. I told you the case is ridiculous. Give it a little time, and it'll toddle off to memory land."

"The hell it will," I said. "I've talked to Ronan. He's in earnest."

"Well, I'm not hiring some legal eagle to fiddle and diddle until he turns this into a case that he can retire on."

"I can put you in touch with a really good lawyer," I said, "who will neither fiddle nor diddle."

"I don't need him."

"Her. Rita Fiore. Used to be a prosecutor."

"She a looker?" Sterling said and smiled and wiggled his eyebrows like Groucho Marx and flicked the ash from an imaginary cigar.

"Oh good," I said. "That'll knock 'em dead in court."

Sterling laughed.

"We'll never get to court," he said. "You can bet your biscuits."

He drank some Chartreuse. Then he lowered his voice and said, "Don't look right now, but there's a man across the street watching us."

"Black man?" I said. "Big, shaved head, shades."

"Yes."

"He's on our side," I said.

"Well, what the hell is he doing over there?"

"Couple of guys came by my office the other day, threatened me if I didn't drop your case."

"Threatened you?"

"Offered me a bribe first."

"And you wouldn't take the bribe."

"Yeah."

"Well, that's damned white of you, Spenser, I must say. Noble, sort of."

"You should probably try to avoid using the word 'white' as an accolade," I said.

"What? Oh hell, Spenser, it's just a damned phrase. So is the Negro a body guard?"

"Not exactly," I said. "I thought it might be useful while I was with you to see if anybody was watching us. Apparently not."

"How can you tell."

"Because if there were someone, you wouldn't see Hawk."

"That's his name?"

"Uh huh. So give me an example of how you kidded these women."

"Boy, you don't give up, do you. Suzy Q got herself a good one."

"Suzy Q?"

Sterling shrugged and laughed and made his little dismissive hand motion.

"I'm glad she got a good one," he said. "She deserves it."

"You touch any of these woman?" I said.

"Hell no."

"They work for you?"

"Haven't we already gone over this ground?" Sterling said.

"I was hoping to find out something this time over," I said.

Sterling grinned at me and sipped his Chartreuse and tipped his head back in pleasure at the taste.

"They work for you?" I said.

"As I mentioned," Sterling said and took any sting out of it by grinning broadly, "these are volunteers. I directed them, in the sense that I was in charge of the whole bubble bath, but none of them was"—he made air quote marks with his fingertips—"working for me."

"So you didn't touch them. You made no sexual innuendoes at them. You didn't use your position of power to create a sexually hostile environment?"

Sterling laughed happily.

"Whoa," he said. "A 'sexually hostile environment'? Holy moley."

"So why did four women suddenly get it into their heads to bring charges against you?" I said.

He got a leather cigar case out of his inside jacket pocket and opened it and offered me one. I shook my head. He took out a long dark cigar and put the case away. With a small pocket knife he trimmed the cigar, put it in his mouth, and lit it carefully, turning it slowly to get the ignition even. When it was going right, he took a big inhale, let the smoke out slowly.

"Maybe it was that time of month," Sterling said, "and they were cranky." Again the big infectious grin to take any sting out of his words. "Do you suppose they threatened you because they know they've got no case?"

"You figure it was the four women who sent the sluggers?" I said.

"Or her husband," Sterling said, looking at the end of his cigar, admiring the glow. "He used to be a criminal lawyer, I heard. He'd probably know somebody."

" 'Her,' meaning Jeanette Ronan," I said.

"Sure."

"Why her rather than, say, Olivia Hanson, or Marcia Albright, or Penny Putnam?"

"By golly, Miss Molly," Sterling said, "you are a detective, aren't you?"

I thought about getting up and going home. I could almost see myself standing and walking off down Newbury Street. I knew if I really could have seen myself walking away I would have looked happy. But I wasn't walking away. I was sitting here trying not to inhale the smoke that spiraled my way from his large cigar.

"How come you focused on Jeanette?" I said.

"She's the one with the husband," Sterling said. "I mean, the other three are currently single, I believe."

He had described them originally, I thought, as the wives of rich husbands. I filed that for future consideration.

"These bad buys actually rough you up?" Sterling said.

"No."

"But they threatened to."

"Yes."

"And they didn't say who they were, ah, representing?"

"No."

"It's got to be Ronan."

"We'll see," I said.

Sterling glanced over at Hawk across the street.

"Why doesn't he join us?" Sterling said.

"I thought you might be more at ease talking alone."

"You're a considerate pilgrim, aren't you."

"Yeah, you want to meet him?"

"Love to."

I gestured to Hawk to join us, and he walked across the street. Hawk always walked in a straight line from where he was to where he was going, and people always got out of his way. He pulled out a chair from another table, turned it around, and sat. He looked at me and shook his head once. No one was following Sterling. I introduced them.

"Good to see ya," Sterling said. "Didn't want you getting lonely over there by yourself."

Hawk looked at Sterling without expression, then looked at me.

"Lonely," he said.

"Want a libation?" Sterling said.

"Champagne be nice."

Sterling gestured at the waiter and ordered. The waiter brought Sterling another Chartreuse, me another beer, and Hawk a bottle of Perrier Jouet in an ice bucket. He poured Hawk a glass and left the bucket handy.

"Seen any bad guys sneaking around Newbury Street?"

I didn't smile, but I wanted to. Hawk was as close to conflicted as he could get. He liked Susan nearly as much as I did, and he knew we were doing this for her and he was determined to be pleasant.

"Just him," Hawk said, pointing at me with his chin.

"He a bad guy?"

"Depends," Hawk said, "if he on your side or not."

"But he's pretty dangerous?"

Hawk smiled. It was an expression of real pleasure. He did his upper class WASP accent where he sounds a lot like James Mason.

"Brad, my man," Hawk said, "you simply have no idea."

"When I was playing football," Sterling said, and I watched Hawk's face go blank again as his attention closed down, "we had some pretty good battles . . ."

Hawk finished his champagne, pulled the bottle from the ice bucket, poured another glass, and drank most of it in a swallow.

thirteen

HAWK'S CURRENT GIRLFRIEND had a town house in the South End, off Clarendon Street close to the Ballet. Susan and Hawk and I were there with her, and maybe fifty of her closest friends, milling about in too little space. The talk was mostly medical, because Andrea was a cardiologist and most of her friends were doctors.

"It's a natural fit," I said to Hawk. "They need patients, you supply them."

"She love me 'cause ah is sensitive," Hawk said.

"Of course she does," Susan said. "Plus your wonderful Amos and Andy accent."

"You'd prefer me to sound like an upward mobile WASP," Hawk said, sounding remarkably like an upward mobile WASP.

"I love you just the way you are," Susan said.

"Anyone would," Hawk said.

Andrea came over in a little red satin dress, carrying a glass of white wine.

"You wear that outfit to work," I said, "you may cause more heart attacks than you prevent."

"Is that a sexist remark?" Andrea said.

"Probably," I said.

"And God bless it," she said. "Hawk, will you please come over here and meet my department head?"

"Impress him," I said to Hawk. "Go with the upward mobile WASP accent."

Andrea stuck her tongue out at me and took Hawk's arm as they walked into the next room.

Susan and I hunkered down in our corner of the party and watched.

"Speaking," Susan said, "of sexism. You haven't told me how things are going with Brad."

"I didn't know that you wanted me to," I said.

"I'm interested, of course."

"Okay. It's kind of a hard one to get hold of. I mean, the charge has been made, apparently the lawsuit is moving forward, but I can't get anybody to tell me what happened, exactly."

"What did you think of Brad?"

"Well, you were right, I kind of like him, but he's either deliberately evasive, or so unfocused that he can't track an idea."

"Like how?"

"I can't get a real sense of whether he harassed these women or not. He's so out of touch with the current standards of male-female propriety that he could have sinned without realizing it."

"What does his lawyer say."

"He hasn't got one."

"Isn't that a mistake, to be faced with a lawsuit and have no lawyer?"

"Certainly. But he says he doesn't want to waste money on a lawyer for a case that isn't going anywhere."

"But how can he be sure?"

"I don't know. He seems entirely unfazed by the whole deal, which seems at odds with the way he presented his situation to you."

"Are you saying I misunderstood?"

"No."

"Because I didn't," she said. "He came to me and said he was desperate. That he had no money. That even if he won, the case would destitute him."

"He says that is not the situation. He says he's doing fine."

"What does he say when you tell him what I told you?"

"He says you were always a little dramatic."

Susan was silent. She swirled her glass of wine and looked at it as if something might be floating in it.

"And how did you respond to that?" Susan said.

"I disagreed."

She looked at her wine some more.

"I hate the image," she said. "Two men sitting around discussing whether I am dramatic."

I nodded. The cocktail party mingled loudly around us. I could see Hawk, taller than most of the room, listening impassively to some guy wearing round gold rimmed glasses, who was making a chopping gesture with his right hand. Probably talking about HMO fee structures.

"Did you get to discuss sleeping with me?" Susan said.

"No."

"I hate this."

"Would you like me to drop it?" I said.

"No."

"Sort of narrows the options," I said.

"Oh don't be so goddamned male," Susan said. "This is very painful. My ex-husband, my current, ah, lover, sitting there talking about me."

"Why?" I said.

"Why? Why wouldn't it be?"

I had a sense that asking why it would be, while symmetrical, wasn't going to get us anywhere.

"Susan," I said. "He doesn't mind that you're with me now. And I don't mind that you were with him then. He appears to like you. I love you. We both speak well of you."

"I don't like it that you speak of me at all."

"I never expected that I would be the only man you had ever been with," I said. "Hell, even after we were together there was Russell."

"Don't speak of him," she said.

"Suze . . ."

"I would like us to pretend that he never happened," Susan said. "That Brad never happened. That there was nothing and no one prior to that snowy Sunday after I came back from San Francisco."

"Isn't that what you shrinks call denial?" I said.

"Denial is when you tell yourself lies," Susan said.

"What is it when we tell each other lies?"

"Why is it a lie not to talk about the other men in my life? I should think you'd be thrilled not to talk about them."

"Everything in your life interests me. There's nothing I mind talking about."

"Well, I do."

"And yet you asked me to save him," I said.

"It doesn't mean we have to talk about it."

I decided that it would also be counterproductive to

remind her that the conversation had started by her asking about Brad.

Instead I said, "Okay with me."

"I couldn't forgive myself," Susan said, "if I let my pathologies contribute to his ruin."

"How about our ruin?" I said.

Susan put her hand on my arm.

"This is a rough patch, and you'll have to help me through it. But nothing can ruin us."

"Good point," I said.

fourteen

I SAT IN THE periodical room at the Boston Public Library reading back issues of the *Globe* and taking notes. Sterling's event at the Convention Center had gotten a lot of press. It had been called Galapalooza. It featured food, drink, celebrities, a message from the President of the United States, and music from a hot singer named Sister Sass. A long list of charities participated and each received a share of the profits. I took down the list of charities, in alphabetical order, and went calling.

The first place was an AIDS support organization operating out of the first-floor front of a three-decker on Hampden Street in Roxbury down back of the Newmarket. The director was a short thin woman with a fierce tangle of blonde hair. Her name was Mattie Clayman.

"You got something says who you are," she said.

I showed her my license.

"So how come a private detective is asking about Galapalooza?"

"I'm trying to investigate a case of sexual harassment that is alleged to have taken place during the production of the event," I said.

Mattie Clayman snorted and said, "So?"

"So I can't get anybody to tell me anything."

"You try asking the victims?"

"I have tried asking everybody. Now I'm asking you."

"I was not sexually harassed," she said.

"I imagine you weren't," I said.

"No? Well, I have been in my life."

"Not twice, I'll bet."

She smiled a little bit.

"Not twice," she said.

"So what can you tell me about Galapalooza?" I said.

"Who is supposed to have harassed who?" she said.

"Brad Sterling is alleged to have harassed Jeanette Ronan, Penny Putnam, Olivia Hanson, and Marcia Albright."

"Busy man," Mattie said.

"You know Sterling?" I said.

"Yep."

"Think he'd have harassed these women?"

"Sure."

"Why do you think so?"

"He's a man."

"Any other reason?"

"Don't need another reason."

"Some of my best friends are women," I said.

"That supposed to be funny?"

"I was hoping," I said.

"There's nothing much to laugh at in the way men treat women."

"How about 'some men treat some women'?"

"You've never been a woman, pal."

"Hard point to argue," I said. "You didn't see any instances of harassment."

"No."

"What else can you tell me," I said. "About Galapalooza?"

She snorted again.

"Something," I said.

She shook her head. "Don't get me started," she said.

"Au contraire," I said. "It's what I'm trying to do."

She made an aw-go-on gesture with her hand.

"How much did you realize from the event," I said.

She looked at me for quite a long time without expression. Finally she said, "Zip."

"Zip?"

"No, actually worse than zip. The people who usually would be giving us money spent it at Galapalooza. So we actually lost the money they would have donated if they hadn't spent it on Galapalooza."

"What happened?" I said.

She shrugged.

"Expenses," she said.

"You see the figures?"

"Yes. Everything was explained," she said. "The costs got ahead of them. The turnout was smaller than they'd hoped."

"So nobody got any money out of it?"

"No."

"Could they have cooked the books?"

"Look at my operation," she said and waved her hand at the small front room of the small apartment that looked out at the narrow street. "Does it look like we have a CPA budgeted?"

"So they could have cooked them."

"Of course they could have cooked them. The deal was that they'd do this big fund-raiser for all the charities too small to do a big fund-raiser. Share mailing lists, pool our volunteers. Because we're small and poor we're in no position to contest their figures. Operations like this are hand to mouth. We scramble every day, for crissake. We haven't got next Monday budgeted."

"Maybe they were just inept," I said.

"Maybe," she said. "Way down below here, where we work, it really doesn't matter if they were inept or dishonest. We don't get money, people die."

I looked at the bare plaster walls, the cheap metal desk and filing cabinet, the curtainless windows with a shirt cardboard neatly taped over a broken pane.

"How long you been doing this work?" I said.

"Ten years."

"If it matters to you," I said, "I will find out what happened and when I do I'll let you know."

"How you going to find out?" she said.

"Don't know yet."

"But you will?" she said.

"Always do," I said.

She put out her hand.

"Maybe you will," she said. "You don't look like someone gives up easy."

I took her hand and we shook.

"You should be proud of yourself," I said. "What you do."

"I am," she said.

fifteen

I TALKED TO some other do-gooders: people who delivered hot meals, people who ran a hospice, people who ran a support group for breast cancer survivors. They were all different, but they had several things in common. They were all tougher than an Irish pizza, their offices were uniformly low budget, and they'd all been screwed by Galapalooza.

It was a really nice day for early spring in Boston, and the temperature was in the sixties when I went to a storefront in Stoneham Square. It was the offices of Civil Streets, the final name on the list I'd culled from the *Globe*, and it was closed. There was a discreet sign in the window that said Civil Streets in black letters on a white background. One of those sorry-we're-closed signs hung in the front door window. The little clock face said they'd be back at 1:15. I looked at my watch. Three fifteen. I looked in through the front window. The place had the impermanent look of a campaign headquarters. A gray metal desk with a phone on it, a matching file cabinet, a couple of folding chairs. I tried the doorknob, nothing ventured, nothing gained. The door was locked. Nothing gained anyway. Maybe they meant 1:15 in the morning. There was a hardware store across the street. I went in and asked the clerk when Civil Streets was usually open.

"It ain't," he said.

"It's not usually open?"

"Nope. Maybe couple hours a week. Some broad comes in, types a little, talks on the phone."

"That's it?"

"That's it," he said.

"What kind of operation is it?" I said.

"I got no idea," the clerk said. "How come you're asking all these questions?"

"I got sick of watching Jerry Springer," I said.

The clerk looked a little puzzled, but he seemed to be a guy who might always be a little puzzled.

"Well, I gotta get to work," he said.

"Sure."

I went back out of the hardware store, walked across the street, and stood and looked at the Civil Streets office. Maybe I should kick in the door and rummage about. Nothing ventured, nothing gained. I glanced around. A Stoneham Police car drove up Main Street and pulled into the parking lot of the hardware store. A cop got out and walked into the store. In a few minutes he came out and stood by his car and gave me a cop look across the street. Cops on a two-man force in East Tuckabum, Iowa, will give you the same you-looking-for-trouble look that prowlies do in the South Bronx. Probably some sort of electro-magnetic force generated by the conjunction of gun and badge. I looked back. He kept looking. Nothing ventured, nobody arrested. I turned and walked back to my car and headed back up Main Street toward Route 128.

The trip wasn't a total waste. I was able to stop at a Dunkin' Donuts near the Redstone Shopping Center and had two plain donuts and a large coffee. Failing to learn anything is hungry work.

Sixteen

RACHEL WALLACE WAS in town. She was teaching a semester at Taft and was giving a lecture this evening at the Ford Hall Forum on Sexual Freedom and Public Policy. I told her if I could skip the lecture I'd buy her dinner. She said the lecture would almost certainly be too hard for me to understand and she'd settle for the meal. So there I was in Julien at the Hotel Meridian where Rachel was staying, sitting in a big chair ordering French food. Rachel Wallace was a pretty good-looking feminist. She had thick black hair, now dusted with a little gray, which she wore shorter than she used to. She had a trim body, and good clothes, and her makeup showed thought and dexterity.

"You still look good," she said when we had ordered our first drink. "If I were heterosexual . . ." She smiled and let it hang.

"Our loss," I said.

The waiter brought her the first of what I knew would be a number of martinis. I had never seen her drunk.

"Are you working on something at the moment?" she said.

"I could probably support myself without working," I said, "but I have joint custody of a dog."

"Of course," she said.

As she always did she checked out the room. And as she usually did she knew somebody.

"Norma," she said to a slender, good-looking woman who was following the maitre d' to her table.

The woman turned, gave a small shriek, and came over to our table. Her husband came with her.

"We haven't seen you since Florida," she said.

Rachel Wallace introduced me. I stood.

"Norma Stilson," she said, "and Roger Sanders."

We shook hands.

"We're coming to see you tomorrow night," Norma said. "We've got tickets."

"I plan to offend a good many people," Rachel Wallace said.

"We wouldn't miss it," Sanders said. "Maybe a drink afterwards."

"Of course," Rachel Wallace said.

They both said they were pleased to meet me and moved on to their table.

"Some people go willingly to hear me," Rachel Wallace said.

"But I'm buying you dinner," I said.

"A transparent attempt to excuse your classic masculine fear of feminism."

"And I did save your life once," I said.

"And you did save my life once," she said. "What are you working on at the moment?"

"I don't think I know."

"What does that mean?"

"It means I can't figure out what the case is about exactly, and the more I look, the more I can't figure it out."

"Tell me," she said.

The waiter brought her a second martini. I was still on my first beer. She wasn't beautiful, but her face had in it such intelligence and decency that it may as well have been beautiful.

"Well, it starts with Susan's ex-husband," I said. "He's a promoter . . ."

"Susan's ex-husband," Rachel Wallace said.

It wasn't a question.

"Yeah."

"Isn't that somewhat, ah, hazardous?" she said.

"It appears to be," I said.

"Susan know you're involved with him?"

"She asked me to do it," I said.

Rachel Wallace drank some martini. She held a swallow in her mouth for a moment. "How do you feel about it?"

"I think it's somewhat hazardous," I said.

"Jealousy?"

"No, I'm all right with it."

"I doubt that," she said. "But I know your capacity for self-control, and I think you can probably do this. On the other hand, I'm not a perfect judge. I think you can probably do anything."

"Me too," I said.

She smiled.

"I know," she said. "Let me speculate for a moment. Let me guess that Susan is having trouble with it."

"She wants me to do it and doesn't want me to do it," I said. "She wants to know what's going on and doesn't want to talk about it. She wants to know what

I think of him and isn't interested in my opinion of him."

"She keep his name?" Rachel Wallace said.

"Yes. But, nice touch, he changed it. To Sterling."

Rachel Wallace smiled. "Lucky his name wasn't Goldman," she said. "What do you think of him?"

"He's kind of a goofball," I said. "Goofy in that way that wealthy old Yankees are sometimes goofy. It's a little hard to describe."

"But of course he's not a wealthy old Yankee," Rachel Wallace said.

"Just pretending," I said. "He's accused of sexual harassment, and he seems to have no interest in it. Susan says he's desperate, broke, facing dissolution. He says he's doing dandy. He ran a big fund-raiser at the Fleet Center last year and nobody got any funds."

"What happened to the money?"

"Don't know. I just found out today that the participating charities got stiffed."

"Sometimes that is simple mismanagement," she said.

"Yep, and Sterling seems capable of it, but a couple of tough guys showed up at my office and threatened to beat me up if I didn't stay away from the case."

"What case?" Rachel Wallace said.

"I guess I'm trying to save Sterling from the sexual harassment charge. Susan says he came to her in desperation."

"What does he say?"

"He says it'll just go away, and by golly he's not a bit worried."

"By golly?"

"By golly."

"But you're wondering about the bad men who

came to call, and about the money that didn't go to charity?"

"Yep."

"And you have a client that says 'by golly.' "

"Sometimes he says 'by golly, Miss Molly.' "

"Please," Rachel Wallace said.

I finished my beer, Rachel Wallace finished her second martini. The waiter brought us each a new drink. I could see Rachel Wallace turning my situation over in her head.

"Either he was pretending to Susan that he was desperate," she said, half to herself, "or he's pretending to you that he's not."

"Or Susan's lying."

"You're just pretending to be objective," Rachel Wallace said. "That she is lying is not a possibility in your universe."

"A fool for love," I said.

"There are worse things to be a fool for," she said. "But don't confuse yourself by pretending you aren't."

"Okay," I said. "You happen to have a working definition of sexual harassment around?"

Rachel Wallace spoke without inflection like a kid saying the pledge to the flag.

"In Massachusetts," she said, "sexual harassment means sexual advances, requests for sexual favors, and verbal or physical conduct of a sexual nature when: (a) submission to or rejection of such advances, requests, or conduct is made either explicitly or implicitly a term or condition of employment or as a basis for employment decisions."

She took in a big stage breath, let it out, drank some martini, and went on. "Or (b) such advances, requests, or conduct have the purpose or effect of unreasonably interfering with an individual's work performance by creating an intimidating, hostile, humiliating, or sexually offensive work environment."

"That's the law?"

"That's it in Massachusetts."

"And you can recite it from memory."

"I'm not just another pretty face," she said.

"Well," I said, "the legislators are clearly a bunch of pickle puss spoilsports."

"Yes," she said. "I understand the Iron Maiden is illegal here too."

"At the moment. But these women were volunteers," I said. "Does the law apply to them?"

"I'm not an attorney," Rachel Wallace said. "But part B might be the more applicable one."

"The thing about the sexually offensive work environment."

She rattled it off again.

"Maybe," I said. "Still, it doesn't seem to me like the strongest case in the world."

"Not every offensive sexual remark is, legally, sexual harassment," Rachel Wallace said. "Have you interviewed the plaintiffs?"

"They won't talk to me, advice of counsel."

"Is the counsel formidable?"

"Francis Ronan?"

"Jesus Christ," Rachel Wallace said.

The waiter offered us menus and we paused to browse them. When we had ordered, Rachel Wallace rested her chin on her folded hands and looked at me.

"Is it difficult with Susan right now?"

"Very," I said.

"Is she ashamed of herself for having been with this man?"

"Maybe," I said. "Though I don't know why."

"I was with you in the last crisis," Rachel Wallace said. "When she went off with that man."

"Costigan," I said. "Russell Costigan."

"As I recall, she was, when it was over, ashamed of herself."

"Well, she was, and she wasn't."

"And with this, ah, Sterling?"

I started nodding before she finished her sentence.

"She is and she isn't," I said.

Rachel Wallace looked enigmatic.

"Which means what?" I said.

Rachel Wallace shrugged.

"You were implying something," I said.

"I'm not a psychiatrist," Rachel Wallace said.

"I'll keep it in mind," I said.

Rachel Wallace scrutinized the olive in her martini for a bit.

"I know of three men in Susan's life," she said. "And they permit ambivalence."

"Three?"

"Her first husband, the man she ran off with, and you."

"Me?"

She turned her glass to get a better look at the olive. Then she looked up at me.

"You look like a thug. You do dangerous work. And, however well contained, you are deeply violent."

"I like dogs," I said.

"Appearances are deceiving," Rachel Wallace said. "And I suspect when Susan first responded to you she didn't realize exactly what she was getting."

"Which was?"

Rachel Wallace smiled. It was a surprising sight.

Her face softened when she smiled, and her eyes widened, and she was pretty.

"A large, cynical Boy Scout," she said.

The waiter brought our dinner.

"She's attracted to men she can be ashamed of?"

"Perhaps."

"You're not just saying that to boost my ego?" I said.

Again that lovely smile.

"You have no ego," she said, "or it is so large it is impregnable. I've never known which."

"But the other two guys, she didn't last with them."

"No."

"With me she has lasted."

"The other two guys," Rachel Wallace said, "were perhaps what she thought they were. You turned out to be more."

"And?"

"She is a good woman, she would finally need a good man."

"And need to be embarrassed," I said, "about the bad ones in her past?"

"Maybe."

"Why?"

Rachel Wallace leaned back a little and rubbed her palms lightly together.

"We have reached the limits of pop psych," she said.

"Which means you don't know."

"I haven't a clue," she said.

"Lot of that going around," I said.

Seventeen

AT 9:15 IN THE morning, I called the Public Charities Division at the Attorney General's Office and asked about Civil Streets. It was listed as a counseling and adjustment service for former prison inmates. The woman on the phone stressed that the description was submitted by the charitable organization and should not be construed as the AG's evaluation. There had been no complaints about the organization. The president was somebody named Carla Quagliozzi, with an address in Somerville. There was a long list of directors: she would be happy to send me a copy of it. I thanked her and hung up and called Civil Streets in Stoneham. No answer. I called President Carla and got a chirpy recorded message about her not being home and my call being important to her. I called Brad Sterling and there was no answer. Faced with rejection at every turn, I went to plan B. I swiveled my chair around and put my feet up and looked out my window. It was a lovely December day, brisk and sunny. Unfortunately it was the first week in April.

Usually when I was puzzled about someone's behavior, I would ask Susan about it. But who to ask when it was Susan's behavior I was puzzled about. Maybe it was time to cultivate another shrink. I thought about what Rachel Wallace had said. It explained why Susan was currently being so difficult. But that didn't mean it was so. Demonic possession would explain it equally as well. But if her theory were valid, it would also mean that Brad Sterling might be a worse guy than he seemed, or that Susan might have thought him so when he was Brad Silverman. She might have been wrong; she misjudged me. Or maybe she hadn't misjudged me. Or maybe Rachel Wallace was all wet.

Across Berkeley Street from my office the windows of the new office building above F.A.O. Schwarz reflected the sun in a blank glare. I thought about Linda Thomas who had once bent over her drawing board in the old building that this one had replaced. A large cloud moved across the sun, cutting the glare off the windows. I could see through them now, but the vista of offices was nearly as blank as the light reflection. The cloud moved quite slowly, and the sun was obscured for a while. But it was a white cloud and the day didn't dim much and after a while it was sunny again.

I checked my watch: 10:20. I called Brad Sterling's office again. No answer. I tried Civil Streets again. No answer. President Carla again. Same thing. I took my feet off the windowsill and put them on the floor and stood and got my coat on and went out.

I got a cup of coffee and a corn muffin on the way and ingested them while I walked up Boylston Street to the Prudential Center. A detective travels on his stomach. I went past the cityscape metal sculpture in the Prudential Building lobby and took the elevator to the thirty-third floor. The office was closed. The door was locked. The receptionist in the marketing company across the hall knew nothing about it. Neither did a bored-looking guy wearing a bad suit in the security office. Neither did I.

In Spenser's Tips For Successful Gumshoe-ing, Tip #6 reads: If nothing is happening and you haven't any idea what you're doing, go someplace and sit and look at something and await developments. Subparagraph A says that most good detectives bring some coffee and a few donuts with them. So I got my car and drove over to Somerville, got some coffee and donuts on the way, and parked in front of Carla Quagliozzi's condo overlooking the Mystic River. Ringing her doorbell got me less than ringing her phone had got me. At least her phone had an answering machine. I leaned on the bell long enough to be sure that if anyone were home they'd have heard it. Then I went back and sat in my car and looked at her house and had a donut while I awaited developments. After an hour or so it occurred to me that I could double the effectiveness of my plan, and I called the Harbor Health Club and asked for Henry Cimoli.

"I need to talk with Hawk," I said.

"Not here."

"Have him call me on my car phone."

"Car phone," Henry said. "You're turning into a fucking Yuppie."

"Quick as I can," I said.

"He know your car phone number?"

"Yes."

"I'll give him the message," Henry said. "You need anything else?"

"Where do I begin," I said.

Henry hung up. And in about twenty minutes Hawk called.

"Do you know what's going on?" I said.

"Almost never," Hawk said.

"Good. I was thinking you could help me not know what's going on."

"You going good on your own," Hawk said.

I explained Spenser's Tip #6, including subparagraph A. Hawk asked me to go slower so he could copy it down.

"I got two very insecure handles on this case," I said. "One is the question of the missing charity money. The other one is the sexual harassment issue."

"You call this thing a case?" Hawk said.

"Verbal shorthand," I said. "What I want you to do is go and sit outside Jeanette Ronan's house and await developments."

"Do I get a big fee?" Hawk said.

"No," I said.

"Do I get donut expenses?"

"Absolutely," I said. "Ask for a receipt."

"Ronans live on Marblehead Neck?"

"Uh huh."

"Might get noticed," Hawk said. "Not that many brothers hanging around out there."

"Dress like a butler," I said.

"Yassah," Hawk said and hung up.

In fact, I knew he'd manage, in ways only he understood, to blend into the scenery in Marblehead just as he did anywhere else. Hawk could infiltrate the Klan if he put his mind to it.

A woman showed up at about two in the afternoon driving a Mercedes sports coupe. She beeped open the garage door to the right of her condo and drove the car into the garage. The garage door slid back down. I waited a moment and got out and walked up her walk and rang the door bell. She still had her coat on when she opened the door. She left the chain bolt in place.

"Carla Quagliozzi, I presume."

"What do you want?" she said.

"I was interested in making a big donation to Civil Streets."

She stared at me without speaking. She was a fleshy young woman with a lot of red hair and a big figure, even with her coat on.

"May I come in?" I said.

"No."

"Are you the president of Civil Streets?"

"Who wants to know?" she said.

"My name is Spenser," I said. "I'm . . ."

She closed the door.

"A private detective," I said to the door. I hate incompletion.

I leaned against her doorjamb for a time and thought about this. She had shut the door on me when she heard my name; I had never said what I was up to. So my name meant something to her. Which meant someone had been talking to her about me, and, given the door slam, warning her not to talk with me. This might be a clue, though I hadn't seen one for so long. I wasn't sure. But if someone had been warning her not to talk to me and I showed up at her door, what would she do next? I walked back to my car and leaned on it. I thought about calling her number to see if the line was busy, but she probably had the accursed call waiting and I wouldn't learn anything.

In about fifteen minutes a dark green Range Rover came around the corner off Mystic Ave and cruised down Shore Drive and parked in Carla's driveway. A guy got out of the driver's side and closed the door carefully behind him and walked to Carla's front door. As far as I could tell, he didn't see me, though he must have because I was standing about ten feet from the driveway. He was taller than I was, with a thin strong look. He was clean shaven. His dark hair was slicked back smooth. He wore a white turtleneck with a black blazer. His sand-colored slacks had a sharp crease in them and his loafers gleamed with polish. He rang the bell, Carla opened the door and let him in. I leaned some more on my car. The caller was in there for maybe twenty minutes and then he came out Carla's front door, closed it carefully behind him, and walked briskly down her walk to where I was leaning. He was a guy used to handling things.

"You're Spenser," he said.

"Yes."

"My name's Richard Gavin," he said. "What was it you wished to talk with Carla about."

"Civil Streets."

"Why."

"Because the AG's office has her listed as the president."

"Don't fuck around with me," Gavin said. "I meant, what did you wish to discuss?"

"Tell me why that's your business," I said.

"Because I've made it my business."

"Good answer," I said.

"Well?"

"I'm looking into a matter tangential to the Galapalooza fund-raiser that Civil Streets participated in last year."

"Yeah?"

"Tangential?" I said.

"What about tangential," Gavin said.

"Aren't you even a little impressed with my use of the word?"

Gavin sighed.

"Okay," he said. "You think you're a funny guy. All your friends think you're a funny guy. Well, I don't think you're a funny guy, you got it? I don't think you're funny even a little bit."

"I'll win you over," I said.

He shook his head.

"What do you want to know about Galapalooza?" he said.

"Civil Streets get any money from it?"

"I'm sorry, that's privileged information."

"The hell it is," I said. "You're a public charity."

"Well, let me be more specific," Gavin said. "That information is privileged to you."

"Just because you don't think I'm funny?"

"Sure," Gavin said. "That'll do."

"This is dumb," I said. "You know and I know that I can find this out. All you do by refusing to tell me is get me wondering why you're refusing."

"It would be in your best interest to leave this alone," Gavin said.

"Because?"

"The 'because' could go two ways," Gavin said. " 'Because you would get a nice bonus if you moved on,' is one way."

"And what would the other way be?"

"Because you could get killed if you don't."

"Ahh," I said. "The old buzz word."

"You're a small-time guy," Gavin said. "And you have put your foot in a big-time puddle. We don't mind. We like to do things easy, if we can. You can walk away from this with a nice piece of change. No problem. Just don't be foolish. Don't get yourself killed because you think you have to be macho man."

"How much?" I said.

"Five large," Gavin said.

"That's a nice bribe," I said. "The trouble is that I am macho man."

"You think you are," Gavin said. "We chew up macho men like M&M's."

"Peanut or plain?"

"Better you should take the money?"

"The thing is, Richard, I hope you don't mind if I call you Richard. The thing is that my entire corporate inventory is a few brains and a lot of balls. I sell that inventory and I'm out of business . . . for five grand."

"And your life," Gavin said.

"Well, sure, that sweetens the pot a little," I said. "But a lot of people have promised to take my life."

Gavin smiled, and put one arm across my shoulders.

"Spenser, I like your style. I really do. But we're a little different maybe than other people you've talked to."

"You going to do it?" I said.

He laughed and took his arm away.

"Well," I said, "it better be somebody better than the two clowns you sent the first time."

Gavin looked puzzled.

"Somebody talked to you already?"

"Big tall fat guy," I said. "And a short thick guy, no neck."

"Not ours," he said.

Gavin had no reason to deny it. And his look of puzzlement had seemed real.

I said, "You haven't seen Brad Sterling around, have you?"

"Who?"

"Just grasping at straws," I said.

"Sure," Gavin said. "So where do we stand?"

"We stand as follows," I said. "A, I'm going to find out what's going on with Civil Streets. And B, don't put your arm on my shoulder again."

Gavin stood and looked at me for a moment. I could see that he wasn't used to rejection. Then he simply turned and left. He walked straight back to his car, got in, started up, and drove away without looking at me again.

Sorehead.

eighteen

SUSAN AND I were running by the head of the
Charles River on the Cambridge side, near the Cambridge Boat Club. It wasn't really the head, it was just
where the river, having encroached north into Cambridge, turned back west toward its birth in Dedham.
But Cambridge is Cambridge and they thought it was
the head.

"Don't get giddy here," I said, "but have you heard
from Brad Sterling?"

"No."

"I went to see him and he wasn't there and his office was closed. Do you know his home address?"

"No."

"You have any thoughts on his absence?"

"Perhaps he's gone away for a few days."

"Perhaps," I said.

The ice was out of the river and the boat crews were
on the cold water pulling hard while their coaches followed in small motor boats, yelling instructions
through bull horns. Susan and I ran with the river on
our left, the sparse Saturday-morning traffic moving

on Fresh Pond Parkway to our right. Across the parkway some kids were out early throwing a baseball on
the prep school field. It was still cold enough so that a
ball off the handle would make your hands ring up to
your shoulder.

Susan ran beside me, on my left, so that my sword
arm would be free. She wore a lavender headband and
gray-lensed Oakley sunglasses and a gray sweat jacket
that said Ventana Canyon on the left breast, and came
low enough to cover most of her fanny, which, she
contended, was ladylike when wearing shiny black
tights. Her running shoes were white with lavender
highlights, which explained the headband. She was in
shape and she ran easily. Me too.

"You work out before you met me?" I said.

"No, I don't think I did," Susan said.

"You play any sports as a kid?"

Susan laughed.

"Cute little Jewish girls, when I was a kid, did not
play sports."

"What did you do," I said.

"We looked beautiful and our daddies took us to li-
braries and theater matinees and movies and museums
and shopping and lunch."

"No mommies?"

"Mommy thought spending money was a bad thing.
She always disapproved of the things my father bought
me."

"Did you have money?"

"We had enough. The drug store did well, I think. I
always thought we were . . . upper class, I guess."

"I bet you were," I said.

We chugged up over the Eliot Bridge and onto the

Boston side of the river. Actually, I chugged. Susan glided.

"It's funny to think of you," I said, "little Suzy Hirsch sitting at dinner every night with these two people that I don't know."

"Thing is," she said, "I didn't know them either."

"Not even your father?"

"Especially my father. He was simply a playmate. He was never really a father. He never reprimanded or instructed, or even explained. If I was doing something he didn't like, he'd speak to my mother about it. She'd do the parenting."

"Which she probably liked," I said.

"Yes, I suppose she did. It gave her status, so to speak, in the family. And it gave her a chance to berate me in a socially acceptable way."

"Probably a lot of parental discipline is disguised anger," I said, just to be saying something. I had no idea what I would accomplish by getting her to tell me about her childhood, but I liked hearing it. And it couldn't hurt.

"Yes, she was quite careful about that. She would denigrate me, whenever she could. If I said something at dinner she would smother a snicker. But every time she did anything direct, she would give it the maternal spin. She had to protect me from my failures of character: 'Oh Susan, you know how you are.' "

"And your father never intervened."

"No. Parenting me was my mother's job. Besides, we had to protect her."

"You and your father."

"Yes."

"From what?"

"From breaking down. She was very nervous. That

was the phrase, nervous. I suppose now we would say she was phobic."

"Oh, Ma," I said. "You know how you are."

Susan smiled.

"Perhaps if you decide to give up professional thuggery," she said, "you could hang out your shingle."

"Then could I say things like, she was projecting her own inadequacies onto you?"

"Yes, only I think you need to deepen your voice a little more and say it more slowly."

There was sweat on Susan's face and sweat had soaked through the back of her gray jacket. But her voice was still even and conversational.

"You and your father ever talk about that?"

"Protecting my mother? No. It was an unspoken agreement. We'd pretend she wasn't phobic. We'd agree that she was 'nervous' and that we didn't want to 'upset her.' But the agreement was silent. We never spoke of it. We never, in my memory, spoke of anything."

"Nothing?"

"Nothing of substance. He'd ask me how I liked school, or tell me what a pretty dress I had on. That sort of thing. But an actual conversation—I can't remember one."

"So the only parent you had was your mother and she was jealous of you. Did she love you too?"

"I think so. I know that I was ashamed of her. She was older than other kids' mothers, and she was really square. And I know I hated her for being so"—Susan smiled sadly—"nervous. But however bitchy she was, I knew she loved me. And she was always there. I trusted her, as much as I despised her. She was the one who took care of me."

"And she had her problems," I said.

"Yes," Susan said, "she had many and they were probably deep seated and my father was probably one of them."

"He fool around?" I said.

"I have no idea," Susan said. "I spent a lot of time with him, but I can't express to you how much I didn't know my father."

From the Harvard Boat House to the Larz Anderson Bridge is uphill. You never notice it driving along Soldier's Field Road. It's not very dramatic, but if it marks the last stretch of a four-mile run, it becomes more apparent.

"Well, dysfunctional or not," I said, "they produced a hell of a daughter."

"A bit dysfunctional herself."

"You think?"

"Not easy to live with," Susan said.

"Impossible to live with," I said. "But what we do works out pretty good."

"Just pretty good?"

"Masculine understatement," I said.

"Oh that," she said.

We went up the little hill and turned left across the Anderson Bridge, where I had almost died last year.

"I am being a bitch," Susan said, "about Brad Sterling."

"Yes."

"I'm sorry."

"I know."

"I don't know if I can promise not to be again."

"I know."

"Nothing breaks you, does it," Susan said. "Nothing makes you swerve."

"For crissake, Suze, I love you," I said. "I plan to continue."

"If I weren't so ladylike," she said, "I might cry."

"Isn't it sort of unladylike, anyway, to sweat like you do?" I said.

"Hey," Susan said. "Unlady-like this!"

"Of course," I said. "How could I have been so wrong."

nineteen

HAWK CAME INTO my office wearing a blue blazer and white trousers.

"Been yachting?" I said.

"Ah is in disguise," Hawk said. "The Marblehead look. Blend right in."

"Boy, you certainly fooled me," I said. "How'd it work?"

Hawk shrugged.

"Been outside the Ronan place maybe an hour when two hard cases come along."

"Cops?"

"Naw. Tough guys. A tall fat one, and a short one with muscles, no neck that I could see."

"Well, well," I said.

"Sound familiar?"

I nodded. "What did they say?"

"They want to know what I'm doing there. And I say, 'Who wants to know?' And they say, 'We do,' and it go sort of like that for a while. And they say if I know what's good for me that I'll haul my black ass out of there."

"That wasn't very sensitive," I said.

"I told them that."

"And?"

"Apparently they hadn't intended it to be sensitive. So, I figured since they looked a lot like two guys braced you a while ago that maybe I might have run into a whatchamacallit . . ."

"A clue," I said.

"That's it," Hawk said, "a clue, and you being a great detective might know what to do with it. So I let them chase me away, and here I am."

"It's the same two guys," I said.

"I figure," Hawk said. "So whoever owns them not only don't want you nosing around, he don't want me."

"He or she," I said.

"That's right," Hawk said. "I was being insensitive."

"I got threatened again yesterday myself," I said.

"Astonishing," Hawk said. "And we so charming too."

"The thing is it was on a matter that Ronan shouldn't have anything to do with."

"You assuming the two stiffs I talked to work for Ronan."

"Yes," I said.

"Sonovagun," he said. "I thought so too, and I not even a great detective. Who threaten you yesterday?"

"Tall guy, sort of thin, strong looking, sharp dresser, drives a dark green Range Rover . . ."

"You got threatened by a guy who drives a Range Rover?"

"Embarrassing, isn't it? Said his name was Richard Gavin."

Hawk shrugged.

"So many assholes," he said. "So little time."

"So I try to find out a little about the alleged sexual harassment and get threatened," I said. "And I ask you to keep an eye on Ronan and you get threatened. And while I'm trying to look into the harassment charges, I find out that Sterling's big charity thing was a bust and nobody got any money. Except that I couldn't get in touch with anyone at a beneficiary group called Civil Streets. So I try to find out a little about Civil Streets because I just stumbled across it while I'm looking into the Sterling thing, and I'm a neat guy, and I like to be thorough, and because I don't know what else to look into, and I get threatened."

Hawk was sitting in one of my office chairs with his feet up on my desk. He was wearing blue suede loafers that matched the blazer.

"I a great detective I might think there was some connection."

"If you were a great detective you might explain to me why Brad Sterling isn't around."

"Gone?"

"I went by there and his office is closed. Nobody knew where he was."

"Secretary."

"Nope. Door was shut and locked."

"It appears," Hawk said, "that the plot be thickening."

"Christ," I said, "maybe you are a great detective."

"Want me to drift by his house, see if he there?"

"Haven't got his address," I said.

"You ask Susan?"

"Yeah."

Hawk nodded. "Here's a trick," Hawk said.

He picked up the white pages from the top of a file

cabinet and riffled through it, and paused and ran his finger down a page and stopped. He shook his head.

"No Bradford Sterling."

"What a shame!" I said. "Watch this."

I punched the speaker phone button and dialed a number and a voice said, "Reilly Research."

"Sean," I said. "Spenser. I need an address."

"Full name," the voice said, "last name first."

"Sterling, formerly Silverman, Brad, I assume Bradford."

"Location?"

"Greater Boston."

"Home or business."

"Home."

"Please hold."

Some Klezmer Muzak came on.

"Klezmer Muzak?" Hawk said.

"Sean thinks it's funny," I said.

"He sounds like a funny guy," Hawk said.

The Klezmer stopped and the voice came back and read out the phone number and an address in Brighton.

"Brighton?" I said.

"Brighton."

I said thank you and the line went dead. I killed the speaker phone.

"Chatty bastard," Hawk said.

"He's a computer geek," I said. "He thinks it makes him seem businesslike."

I turned the speaker phone back on and called the number in Brighton. After four rings a machine answered.

"Hi, Brad Sterling. Sorry I'm not here right now, but your call is important to me, so please leave a message and I'll call you back as soon as I can."

I hung up.

"Why would he have an unlisted number?" I said.

"Everybody got unlisted numbers," Hawk said. "It's one of the ways you know you a Yuppie."

"I suppose you're in the promotion business you don't want people calling you at home," I said. "You in on this deal?"

"Uh huh."

"There's nothing in it for either one of us."

"Susan might like it," Hawk said.

"Not so far," I said.

"But she might," Hawk said. "Later on."

"Maybe," I said.

"Besides," Hawk said, "I made two hundred thousand last week in Miami, so I can afford to take a few days, and I don't much like people threatening me."

I did not ask him what he had done in Miami to earn the money.

"Okay," I said. "Let's go over and burgle Sterling's apartment."

"What you looking for?"

"I have no idea," I said.

"It's a start," Hawk said.

twenty

STERLING'S APARTMENT WAS a second-floor walk-up on a middle-class street off Commonwealth Avenue, before you got to Washington Street, just this side of Brookline. Hawk was not impressed.

"Maybe Brad ain't as rich as he say."

We'd come properly equipped, which is a definite advantage for B&E, the pry bar and other things in a red Nike gym bag. It took us about ninety seconds to jimmy the door quietly enough so that nobody stuck their head out into the hall and said "hey"; and neatly enough so that when we closed it behind us the break-in wasn't obvious.

It was one room and sparsely furnished. Narrow bed, clean sheets, neatly made, table and chair, bureau, bath off one side, no kitchen. A long hook swung out from the back of the door for suits and sport coats to hang on, and a single window looked out on the air shaft. Hawk was even less impressed.

"Maybe Brad a lot less rich than he say."

"Maybe he simply prefers Thoreauvian simplicity," I said.

"Sure," Hawk said. "That probably it."

"Lucky Susan's not still married to him," I said.

"She don't prefer Thoreauvian simplicity," Hawk said.

"No."

Searching the place wasn't a challenge. Our only problem was that it was so small we got in each other's way. Brad was a neat guy. His socks were carefully rolled. His freshly laundered shirts were organized by color. His spare keys were in a small lacquer box, each key neatly labeled with little plastic tags. There was nothing very interesting about the labels. I put the keys in my coat pocket and put the box back in the drawer. Neckties lay on top of the bureau as neatly as in a haberdashery case. Three pairs of shoes were lined up under the foot of the bed. Under the head of the bed was a working flashlight, and a box which had once contained a pair of Rockport walking shoes. Now it contained a thick bundle of letters, still in their envelopes. Hawk dumped the box out on the bed and we each took a letter. The letters were handwritten in bright purple ink on lavender stationery in what I took to be a female hand. They were all addressed to Brad Sterling at this address. We each read our letter. The salutation was "My darling."

"If I wasn't such a dangerous and self-contained African American person," Hawk said, "I'd blush."

"Like me," I said.

"Just like you, 'cept the flush be darker. You know who writing these letters?"

"Mine is signed 'J,' " I said.

"Mine too," Hawk said.

"Could be Jeanette," I said.

"Like Jeanette Ronan?"

"Like that," I said. "Or it could be Jane, or Janet, or Jean, or Jenny, or some private lover's nickname that we couldn't even guess."

"Life be easier if it's Jeanette," Hawk said.

We read some more letters. All starting "My darling." All of them signed "J."

"She not too inventive," Hawk said. "But she very concrete."

"This is less fun than you'd think it would be," I said.

The room had a stuffy, closed-up feel as we stood reading the mail.

"You the expert here," Hawk said. "You call these love letters?"

"She says she loves him," I said.

"That ain't what she spends her time talking about," Hawk said.

"It's a white thing," I said.

In the fifth envelope I picked up, tucked neatly inside the folded stationery, was a Polaroid picture.

"Jeanette Ronan," I said and held the picture up for Hawk to see. Jeanette was naked, standing smiling in front of a canopied bed.

"All of Jeanette Ronan," he said. "Guess life going to be easier for once."

"I wonder who took the picture?" I said.

"Say in the letter?" Hawk asked.

I read the letter. It alluded to the picture and was very detailed in what the naked woman pictured had in mind for the recipient. But it didn't tell me who took it.

"No," I said and handed the letter to Hawk.

He read it carefully. "You know, I never thought of doing that," he said.

"Hang around," I said. "You learn."

"Maybe 'My darling' took the picture," Hawk said.

"It's a Polaroid. If he took it, then why did she mail it to him?"

"So you think somebody else taking nudies of her?" Hawk said. "And she mailing them to 'My darling'?"

"That may be the definition of depravity," I said.

"Or thrift," Hawk said. "Two for one."

"Sometimes your cynicism achieves Shakespearean resonance," I said.

"Coming from you," Hawk said, "that a real compliment."

We continued through the letters. We found three more photographs of Jeanette Ronan nude. No useful explanation in the letters, though the pictures were mentioned. When we got through, we put everything back the way it was and closed up the shoebox. I put the shoebox in the gym bag.

"Look like sexual harassment to you?" Hawk said.

"Maybe she's harassing him," I said.

"How many straight single guys you know feel harassed by getting nude pictures of good-looking women in the mail?" Hawk said.

"Just a thought," I said.

There was a phone on the top of the bureau with an answering machine beside it. I went over and pushed the all-message play button. The first message began without preamble.

"Brad you sonovabitch," a woman's voice said. "You either send the goddamned support payment or I swear to Christ I'll have you back in court."

"Reach out and touch somebody," Hawk said.

"Hi Brad," another woman's voice. "It's Lisa. I'm feeling neglected. Call me."

We listened to all thirteen calls, the mechanical machine voice announcing time and day of call after each one. The calls spanned at least a week. Two were from the Brighton branch of DePaul Federal Savings asking him to please call. One was from an outfit called Import Credit Company in regard to his car lease payment, please call. There was a call from the Cask and Carafe Wine Shop saying that his check had been returned and asking when he could come in and settle his account. Another angry call about money. Another call from Lisa, this one more urgently wondering why he hadn't called. "I don't want to think I'm just another notch on your gun," she said. Five other calls from women following up on a recent evening, or looking forward to one in the offing.

I wrote down all the names.

"Brad seems to have mixed success with women," I said.

"But not from lack of trying," Hawk said.

"And he's living in one room in Brighton," I said, "and not paying his bills."

"So, unless he very thrifty," Hawk said, "the story he told Susan is right."

"Sounds near dissolution to me," I said.

"You find an address book anywhere?" Hawk said.

"No."

"Checkbook?"

"Nope."

"Maybe his office," Hawk said.

I reached in my coat pocket and took out the keys and found the one marked office.

"Maybe," I said.

twenty-one

THE FIRST THING we noticed when we went into Sterling's office was the smell. Hawk and I looked at each other. We both knew what it was. I closed the office door behind us and fumbled for the light switch, and found it to the right of the door, and turned on the lights. There was nothing unusual in the outer office. The door to Sterling's private office was closed. As I opened it I was already dreading what I'd find, and dreading telling Susan about it. I turned on the lights. The body was there, facedown on the rug in front of Sterling's desk, a wide black soak of blood showing on the rug under him, the head turned at an angle only death permitted. I turned on the light. The smell was bad. The body had begun to bloat. I didn't want to look. I held my breath and went and squatted on my heels and looked at the face. It wasn't much of a face anymore. It wasn't much of anything anymore. But it wasn't Sterling. I stood and breathed again, trying not to breathe through my nose.

"Not Sterling," I said.

"Anybody we know."

"I don't know him."

Hawk bent over and stared at the corpse for a moment.

"Nope," he said and walked to the desk and turned on the lamp.

"We're going to have to toss the place," I said.

"I know."

"I'll take this office," I said. "You do the outer."

"You know what you're looking for?" Hawk said.

"Clues."

I took two pairs of disposable latex gloves from the Nike bag and gave one pair to Hawk. We put them on. There was a computer on Sterling's desk. I turned it on. It was a Mac, like Susan's. I clicked open the hard drive. There were twenty-six items on the hard drive including a folder marked "Addresses." I opened the drawers in Sterling's desk and found some blank disks. I put one in the computer and copied the hard disk onto it. I put the copy on the desk and shut off the computer. I went through Sterling's desk. I concentrated on breathing through my mouth, and on avoiding eye contact with the corpse. I found no checkbook. The bottom right drawer had a lock. I found a key for it among the ones I'd taken from Sterling's apartment. In the drawer was a narrow case made of gray translucent plastic. In the case were a dozen disks. I took the case out of the drawer and left the drawer unlocked. I added the copy of the hard disk I had made and put the whole thing in the Nike bag on the desktop. I got on my hands and knees and looked under the desk. I turned the desk chair upside down and looked at the underside of it. I rummaged through the wastebasket. I ran my hand over the door frame and felt under the edges of the rug. Feeling under the rug got me closer to the corpse than

I wanted to be. I stood up and went and checked the windows. They didn't open. I paused in a corner of the office away from the corpse and surveyed the room. It was a suspended ceiling and a thorough search would include looking behind it, and in the ventilation ducts. But that was too much time invested for what it was likely to earn me. I wanted to see what I had on the disks and I didn't want any cops showing up and taking them away from me. I went to the desk and got the Nike bag and detoured around the corpse into the outer office.

"Anything?" I said.

Hawk was sitting on Patti's desk, still wearing the sanitary gloves.

"Usual stuff," Hawk said. "Invoices, receipts, letters, promotional material. Only thing interesting is what I didn't find."

"Which is?"

"Civil Streets," Hawk said. "There is nothing with their name on it. No file, no letters, no bills, nothing. You find his checkbook?"

"No."

"So wherever he went, he took it with him."

"Yep, and we know he's got one because one of those phone messages was about a bounced check."

"How you feeling?" Hawk said.

"I haven't thrown up yet," I said.

"Good to work with a pro."

"Even better to work out here where the smell isn't as strong," I said.

"Okay. There's that," Hawk said. "You want to wipe down the door knobs and the light switches."

"No. It's reasonable that my fingerprints would be there."

"You calling the cops?"

"Yes."

"Law abiding," Hawk said.

I took off the gloves and dropped them into the Nike bag. I put the spare keys in there too, except the one for the office.

"Hang onto these," I said.

"Law abiding, but not crazy," Hawk said.

"I'll be in touch," I said. "When the cops get through yelling at me."

Hawk smiled, took the Nike bag, and went out the office door, leaving it open behind him. I waited five minutes for him to clear the building, then I dialed up Martin Quirk.

twenty-two

I SAT IN Patti's chair in the outer office for maybe an hour and a half waiting for Quirk to get to me. Quirk hadn't changed much since he made captain. He still showed up at most crime scenes. He spent too much time investigating and too little time managing the department, which was why it took him so long to make captain in the first place, and why a lot of the hierarchy wanted to replace him. And I knew that he cleared more cases than any commander in the department, which was why the hierarchy couldn't replace him. If Quirk knew any of this, he paid no attention to it.

Finally it was my turn.

"You know how to give a statement," Quirk said. "Christ knows you've done enough of them."

He and I were sitting together in the outer office, Quirk on the corner of Patti's desk, me still in her chair, which was too small. Quirk's employees had photographed the corpse and now were dusting for fingerprints, and measuring, and sampling, and poking, and studying. A team from the coroner's office finished getting the remains into a body bag and onto a gurney. They trundled it past us as we sat, leaving behind only the blood-stained rug, a chalk outline, and the strong smell.

"Well," I said. "First of all you'll find my fingerprints on the door and the light switches and the phone."

"I sort of guessed that," Quirk said. "And I'm also guessing that we won't find them anywhere else."

"Of course not," I said.

"Which will not mean that you didn't touch anything else."

"Boy, have you gotten cynical," I said, "since you made captain."

Quirk rarely smiled, and he didn't this time, but his gaze, which was always steady, rested on me a little more lightly than it sometimes did.

"Go on," he said. "Tell me your story."

So I did, as best as I could, since I didn't understand it too well myself. I left out any mention of searching Sterling's apartment. Quirk listened without expression. His thick hands rested quietly on his thighs. He always dressed well. Tonight he had on a blue tweed jacket and a white button-down shirt with a blue knit tie and gray slacks. He never needed a haircut. He always looked clean-shaven. His shirts were always freshly laundered. His plain toe cordovan shoes were always shined. When I got through explaining myself, Quirk was silent for a time.

Then he said, "Susan's ex-husband?"

"Yes."

He was silent again for a time. Then he shook his head slowly. I shrugged.

"And this is his office," Quirk said after a while. "To which he gave you a key."

"Yes."

"Because he thought it might be convenient for you to come here and let yourself in."

"Right," I said.

Quirk looked at me some more.

"We both know that's horseshit," he said. "But we also know that's all you're going to say until there's reason to say something else."

"Captain, you can't mean that," I said.

"I know you long enough to know how many corners you'll cut," Quirk said. "But I also know you end up most of the time on the right side of the way things work out."

I looked at him openly and honestly and didn't say anything.

"And"—Quirk almost smiled—"you got enough problems for the moment." He shook his head. "Susan's ex. Jesus Christ."

"You don't know who the stiff is?" I said.

"White male."

"Driver's license, anything?"

Quirk almost made a face.

"Coroner's people will go through the body," he said.

"Don't blame you," I said. "Coroner say anything about time of death."

"A while ago," Quirk said. "They get him to the lab, they'll be more exact."

"Cause of death?"

"Gunshot. Probably a small caliber. In the chest, doesn't seem to be an exit wound. We assume it's still in him."

"So he was facing whoever shot him."

"Yep. And he was carrying. When they were getting him in the bag there was a gun under him. Colt Python."

"So he had it out," I said.

"Not quite soon enough," Quirk said.

"So maybe he wasn't just somebody stopped by to organize an event," I said.

"Lot of people carry guns these days," Quirk said.

"The American way," I said. "You'll let me know when you get an ID?"

"Sure," Quirk said. "That's how we like to operate. We tell you everything we know. You bullshit us. You don't know where your client is now, I suppose."

"No I don't."

"You find out maybe you could give me a jingle?"

"Of course," I said.

Quirk did not look as if he believed me entirely.

"You think he shot this guy?" he said.

"His office," I said. "And he's disappeared."

"We noticed that too."

"Doesn't mean he did it," I said.

"Doesn't mean he didn't," Quirk said.

"Mind if I go," I said.

"Go ahead," Quirk said.

I was tired. I walked slowly out through the uniformed cops standing around in the corridor and got in the elevator and went down. I looked at my watch. It was 3:40. When I went outside it was raining. Boylston Street was empty. The wet pavement gleamed under the street lights, reflecting the bright lifeless color of the neon signs that gleamed an artificial welcome outside bars and restaurants closed for the night. I turned up my coat collar and trudged down Boylston Street, thinking about the most encouraging way to tell Susan that her ex had upgraded from sexist to murder suspect. The rain came harder. This thing showed every sign of not working out well for me.

twenty-three

SUSAN HAD HER first appointment at eight. Normally I never called her before she went to work, because she was zooming around like the Flight of the Bumble Bee, getting ready. Years ago I had stopped asking stupid questions, like why not start getting ready earlier so you won't be so rushed? And when I was there in the morning, I sat at the kitchen counter and had coffee and read the paper so as not to get trampled. But this morning I didn't want her to hear from television about the corpse in Sterling's office. They probably didn't have it yet, but I didn't want to take the chance. So soggy with two hours' sleep I turned off my alarm and rolled over in bed and called her up and told her what I knew.

"Do you know where Brad is?" Susan said.

As always, about important stuff Susan was calm. It is about the small stuff that she permits herself frenzy.

"No. He's not at home, or at least he wasn't last night."

"Do you think he is in trouble?"

"Yes," I said.

"Do you think he killed the man?"

"Don't know," I said. "He's obviously a suspect."

"Do you want to get out of this?"

"Not unless you want me to."

She was quiet on the phone for a moment. "No, if you are willing, I'd like us to see it through."

"I'm willing," I said.

"When will I see you?" Susan said.

"After your last patient," I said. "I'll buy you dinner."

"Sevenish," Susan said.

Unless she had to, Susan never specified an exact time. Since I never knew how to time an arrival at sevenish, I always specified, knowing I'd wait anyway.

"I'll be there at seven," I said.

"Maybe you ought to try and go back to sleep," she said. "You were up awfully late."

"Good suggestion," I said.

"Yes," she said.

There was a pause.

Then she said, "And thank you."

"You're welcome," I said.

I knew the thank you covered a lot of ground. It didn't need to be exact.

Showered, shaved, wearing a crisp white shirt, with my jeans pressed and new bullets in my gun, I arrived at the office a little past noon, carrying a ham and egg sandwich and two cups of coffee in a brown paper bag. I took off my raincoat and my new white Red Sox cap, sat at my desk, and ate my sandwich and drank my coffee with my office door invitingly open and my feet up on the desk so anyone going by could see that I had some new running shoes. Except for the fact that I had absolutely no idea what I was doing, I was the very model of a modern major shamus. After I finished my sandwich and the first cup of coffee, I considered what options the day offered. I decided that the best one was to drink the second coffee, which I had commenced to do when Hawk showed up carrying the red Nike gym bag. He took two coffees out of the bag and put them on the edge of my desk and sat in a client chair and put the gym bag on the floor.

"Want another coffee?" he said.

"Absolutely," I said. "Doubles my options."

"Got your computer disks," he said.

"Good," I said. "Give us something to do."

"What's this 'us'?"

"You're not computer literate?"

"Been keeping company," Hawk said. "With a woman works for a software outfit. One night she show me the wonders of the Internet."

"Your reward probably for being such a studly," I said.

"Studly be its own reward," Hawk said. "Anyway, that more than I want to know about computers."

"You don't groove on the information highway?"

Hawk snorted.

"What I like," I said, "is how this wondrous artifact of science is primarily useful as a conveyance for dirty pictures."

"Of ugly people," Hawk said.

"Sadly," I said.

"Confirms your faith," Hawk said.

"My faith is unshakable, anyway," I said.

Hawk reached into the gym bag and produced a white paper bag, from the white paper bag he produced a donut. He took a bite of the donut and leaned forward and put the bag on the desk.

"Now here's a real bridge to the twenty-first century," I said and took a donut.

"Quirk tell you anything last night?" Hawk said.

"They hadn't ID'd him yet," I said. "Nobody wanted to search the body."

"Let the ME do it," Hawk said.

"That's what Quirk said. Stiff had a gun, though. It fell out of his pocket when they were taking him away."

"So maybe he ain't from the United Way," Hawk said.

"Or maybe he is," I said.

I swung my chair around so I looked out my window. It was still raining, which in Boston, in April, was not startling to anybody but the local news people who treated it like the Apocalypse. I liked the rain. It was interesting to look at, and I enjoyed the feeling of shelter on a rainy day. When I was a little kid in Wyoming, the darkened days outside the school room window had given me something to contemplate while I was being bored to death. Something about its implacable reality reminding me that school was only a temporary contrivance. While I was thinking about the rain, the morning mail came. There was a check from a law firm I'd done some work for. There was some junk mail from a company selling laser sighting apparatus for hand guns. I gave the brochure to Hawk. And there was a letter from the Attorney General's Public Charities woman with a list of the principals involved with Civil Streets. With my feet propped against the windowsill I went through the list. It told me that Carla Quagliozzi was president and gave me her address. I already knew that. It listed a number of people on the board of directors, none of whom I knew, except

Richard Gavin. His address was Gavin and Brooks, Attorneys-at-Law, on State Street. Son of a gun. I sat for another moment thinking about that. Behind me I heard Hawk crumple the brochure on laser sights and deposit it in the wastebasket beside my desk. I looked at the rain for a while longer.

"Okay," I said and swung my chair back around and got up and walked over to the narrow table that ran along the left-hand wall of my office. There was a computer on it. I turned it on.

"Gimme the disks," I said.

twenty-four

I AM INEXPERT with a computer and hope to remain so. I had bought one initially because Susan had one and took to it easily and had become almost immediately convinced that no office should be without one. When I did use the computer, which was rarely, and I ran into a problem, which was whenever I used the computer, I called Susan and she straightened me out. Today I ran into a problem at once. When I started up the computer and slipped in a copy of Sterling's hard disk, I couldn't get any of the folders open. I tried the other disks from the disk file we'd taken from Sterling's office. Everything was locked. Hawk was sitting in my chair with his feet up on my desk watching me.

"Need a code," he said.

"Thank you, Bill Gates," I said.

"Trying to be helpful," he said.

"Consultants!" I said in a loud mutter.

Susan did not seem the appropriate resource in this case, so I got up and went to my desk and called Sean Reilly.

"I've got some disks," I said, "that I can't get open."

"Locked?"

"I assume so."

"I'll come over."

I said thank you, but he had already hung up.

"Help is on the way," I said.

"He going to bring donuts," Hawk said.

"I don't think Sean ever ate a donut," I said.

"Then how much help he going to be?"

Reilly arrived in about ten minutes, which was the time he took to carry his black plastic briefcase down Boylston Street from the Little Building where he had an office. He walked in, gave me a brief nod, and sat down at the computer table. I introduced Hawk. Sean gave him a brief nod as he opened the briefcase and took out some software.

"You related to Pat Riley?" Hawk said, his face blank.

"No."

Sean was a medium-sized, mostly bald guy, with a patchy ineffective beard. The thin fringe of long hair that remained around the perimeter of his head was not much more effective than the beard. He wore a red plaid flannel shirt, the collar of which was folded out over the double-breasted lapels of a gray sharkskin suit. On his feet were green rubber boots with brown leather tops, in deference, I hoped, to the rain. He slid a disk into the computer and leaned forward looking at the screen. His hands moved over the keyboard as if he were playing Mozart.

"Unlock everything?" Sean said.

"Yep."

He ejected the first disk and slipped in another one,

his gaze still locked onto the screen. He nodded as if to affirm a truth.

"Take about half an hour," he said.

"Fine."

He paused. We waited. He stared at the screen without moving.

Finally he said, "I don't like people watching me."

"Ahh," I said.

Hawk and I got up and went out and leaned on the wall in the corridor.

"People normally kick you out your own office?" Hawk said.

"Just artists," I said.

Hawk said, "Sean on his way to a costume party, you think?"

"I told you, he's a computer geek," I said. "To him that's dress-for-success."

We loitered in the hall another twenty minutes, while Sean Reilly practiced his black arts. Hawk took the opportunity to brush up on his surveillance skills by watching the receptionist in the design office across the hall.

"Are you objectifying that young woman?" I said.

"Absolutely not," Hawk said. "I thinking about her with her clothes off."

"Oh," I said. "No problem there."

My office door opened, Reilly came out, carrying his ugly briefcase.

"Files are open. Bill's on your desk," he said and walked off down the corridor.

"Nice talking to you," Hawk murmured.

We went back into the office and I sat down at my computer. I put in the hard disk copy I had made and clicked open a folder marked "Addresses." It blossomed before me as if kissed by a summer rain.

Susan's address was there, and mine, and Carla Quagliozzi and someone named Lisa Coolidge, who may or may not have been worried about being another notch on Brad's gun, and a number of people whose names meant nothing to me. And Richard Gavin.

"I go see Carla Quagliozzi," I said to Hawk, who was still leaning back in my chair with his feet up and his eyes closed. Hawk could sit motionless, as far as I knew, for days. "She's the president of Civil Streets. And Richard Gavin shows up and leans on me. I get a list of directors of Civil Streets from the AG's office and Richard is on it. We open up Sterling's address book and there's Richard."

"Say what he does?" Hawk said.

"Apparently he's a lawyer."

"Oh good," Hawk said.

"Yeah, not many of them around," I said.

I went back to the computer. Jeanette Ronan was there and all the other women who were alleging sexual harassment. There was a woman named Buffy, no last name, there were a number of women. I took some notes.

When I finished with the addresses, I closed them and opened a folder titled "Finance." Some of it was simple. There was a list of names under the heading: Monthly Nut. The name Buffy was listed and beside it $5,000/mo. Cask and Carafe, $600/mo. Matorian Realty, $1,100/mo. Import Credit, $575/mo. DePaul Federal, $4,000/mo. Foxwood School, $22,000/year. Then there was a notation, "Galapalooza—see blue disk."

"So why would he bother to lock this information," I said.

"What's a blue disk?" Hawk said.

"No idea," I said.

"Maybe stuff on blue disk was on this disk once," Hawk said. "And he coded it. Then later on he change it onto the blue disk and didn't take the code off."

"Be nice if we had the blue disk," I said.

"Bc nicc if wc had lunch," Hawk said.

"Well, hell," I said. "There's something we can find."

And we did.

twenty-five

SUSAN AND I went up to Essex and had some fried clams at a place called Farnham's. We got the clams, and some onion rings to go, and ate them in the car looking out over the tidal marshes toward Ipswich Bay. It was still raining. And it was cold enough to leave the car running and the heater on low. I had brought with me some Blue Moon Belgian White Ale in a cooler, and a jar of tartar sauce. Farnham's sold beer and they gave you little cups of tartar sauce for free. But Blue Moon Belgian White was a little exotic for Farnham's, and it always took too many little cups for the proper clam-to-tartar-sauce ratio. Susan watched me as I arranged the tartar sauce and the Belgian White, to be ready at hand.

"You don't leave much to chance, do you?" she said.

"Proper provisioning is the mark of a good eater," I said.

I had a large order of clams. Susan had chosen the small. We shared an order of rings. Sharing with Susan was always good because she consumed slowly and not too much. We ate for a time in silence. The evening had darkened and the windshield wipers were off so that we couldn't see much of the scenery and what we could see was blurred. But the lights from the clam shack made dark crystal patterns out of the rain that sluiced on the windshield, and the steady sound of the rain made the dark interior of the car seem like the perfect refuge.

"Police have any leads on Brad," Susan said.

"Not that they are sharing with me."

"Were we going to share those onion rings?" Susan said.

"Of course," I said. "I was only picking out the fattening ones to save you."

"And so fast," Susan said.

"Just doing my job, little lady."

I got the right amount of tartar sauce on a clam and put it in my mouth.

"Brad always had to be a success," Susan said.

I chewed my clam.

"No, it's not quite that," Susan said.

She was staring out at the barely discernible tidal marshes, her profile lit by the lights from the clam shack.

"He always had to be perceived as a success," she said.

"You would have helped," I said.

"Or he thought I would," she said.

I ate another clam.

"Could he really have shot someone?" she said.

It seemed a rhetorical question to me. Even if it wasn't, I decided to treat it like one. I examined my clams and my tartar sauce to make sure I wasn't getting disproportionately ahead in one area or the other.

"You think?" she said.

"I don't know, Suze. I barely know him."

"Hell, I probably don't know him any better," Susan said.

She ate half a clam, no tartar sauce. She said she hated tartar sauce. She had always hated tartar sauce, and no amount of psychotherapy had ever succeeded in changing her.

"I was married to him a lifetime ago," Susan said. "One of the common problems I run into in the shrink business is the assumption that people are always what they were. That time and experience haven't changed them."

"It's the basis of reunions," I said.

"Reunions are normally a fund-raising device," Susan said, "contrived by the sponsoring institution to exploit that delusion."

"And it makes you mad as hell," I said.

"I suppose so," Susan said. "It stunts people's growth."

"Mind if I have another ring?" I said.

"Speaking of growth . . . No, go ahead. I won't be able to eat my share anyway."

"Could the Brad you were married to have shot somebody?"

"I always thought he was weak," Susan said. "He covered it. He was big, he played football. He became more Harvard than the Hasty Pudding Club—of which he was a member, by the way."

"Lucky duck," I said.

"But he didn't seem to have any real inner resources. You couldn't trust his word. You couldn't count on him. One reason I didn't want children is that I couldn't imagine him being a good father. I couldn't imagine him working at whatever job he had to because his kids needed to be fed. I couldn't imagine him actually being a man. I would have said he didn't have the courage to shoot someone."

"Doesn't necessarily take courage," I said. "Weakness would do. Fear. Desperation."

"Yes," Susan said, "of course."

She smiled. I could tell she was smiling as much from the sound of her voice as I could from the look of her face in the rain-dimmed car. It didn't sound like a happy smile.

"Did he have a gun when you knew him?" I said.

"I don't think so, but it would have been a nice accessory for his self-esteem."

"Which was a little shaky," I said.

"Yes."

"Was he in the army?"

"No."

"Does the name Buffy mean anything to you?"

"I think she was my successor," Susan said.

"Carla Quagliozzi?"

"No. Brad's been married several times; I only knew the next woman. But you must understand that the Brad I knew needed to be with a woman. Since many women would find him initially attractive, but finally insufficient, I imagine there have been quite a few."

"His parents alive?"

"No."

"You mentioned a sister, went to Bryn Mawr."

"Yes, Nancy."

"Know where she is?"

"Bedford. She's married to a dentist."

"Know her married name."

"Ginsberg."

"I guess she's not trying to pass," I said.

Susan didn't comment. She ate a clam instead.

"Any other family," I said.

"He has children," Susan said, "from other marriages. I don't know anything about them."

We finished our supper. I got out and emptied the clam cartons and other debris into the trash barrel. The rain seemed a little harder now, and the wet smell of it mingled with the strong smell of the salt marsh. I stood for a minute and smelled it, and felt the rain, and looked at the swamp water, its obsidian surface dappled by the rain. Then I took a deep breath and got back in the car.

"Obviously none of my business," I said. "And obviously a sore spot, but if you knew what he was, why did you marry him?"

Susan didn't reply for a while. I could see her imposing control on herself. I knew her so well I could think along with her. Hard questions were part of what she did every day. If she could regularly ask them, she ought to be able to answer one or two. And even though the question was out of line, she had opened the door to all of this by inviting me in that evening when we sat in the Bristol Lounge listening to music and liking each other. She imposed patience upon herself and it showed in the tone of her answer.

"Of course I didn't know his failures when I married him," she said. "He seemed a great catch. Football player. Big man on campus. Money in the family. I learned of his shortcomings during our marriage and finally they were enough to cause our divorce."

"How about me?" I said.

"Excuse me?"

"What was there about me that made you love me, besides my reputation as a world-class lover?"

"I didn't know that about you," she said.

"But you soon learned, didn't you, my proud beauty."

"Oh my," she said.

"But besides that?"

"I've never thought about it," she said.

"Aren't you in the think-about-it business?" I said.

"About other people," she said softly.

I waited. This was risky. But the whole thing was risky. If I was going to help her get through this, I needed her to think about herself. She was smart as hell, and she was tough as hell, and if she thought about herself in this context for a while good things would emerge . . . Maybe. The rain came down hard on the roof of the car. A station wagon with fake wood sides pulled in beside us and a man and woman and three children piled out and scooted through the rain for Farnham's. Far out at the edge of the salt marsh I could see the running lines of a power boat as it edged along toward where Hog Island would have been had the day been sunny and clear. I waited. Me and Carl Rogers.

"You were, are, the most dangerous person I've ever known," she said.

"That was it?"

"I don't know. That's what seems to bubble up when I think about you. I'd never met anyone like you. You were obviously a good man, and you were nice, and I found you attractive, but you were so dangerous," she said.

"So it wasn't just my open Irish punim."

"No."

"Did you know that when you, ah, consummated our relationship?"

"I knew it the second time around."

"After Russell," I said.

"No, after Dr. Hilliard."

"The San Francisco shrink."

"Yes. It was Russell's attraction too."

"I turned out not to be dangerous enough?" I said.

She shook her head. "Not that," she said.

"What?"

She shook her head again and didn't speak.

"You want to stop talking about this?"

"Yes."

So we did.

On the drive home, she seemed to go quite deep inside herself. I sang all the lyrics to "Lush Life" for her and she didn't even ask me to stop.

twenty-six

I TALKED WITH Nancy Ginsberg at ten in the morning in the living room of her semi-colonial home which attached via the garage to another semi-colonial home with which it shared a one-acre lot in a development called Bailey's Field in Bedford.

The room was bright. The colors were quiet and co-ordinated. The pieces of furniture went together calmly. There was a piano in one corner of the room and a large color photograph of the children, two boys and a girl, sat on top of it. There was a fireplace on the back wall, faced in gray blue slate. It was clean and new and looked as if no flame had ever soiled it.

Nancy was appropriate to the living room. She had on a pink cashmere sweater, a single strand of pearls, a gray wool skirt, and low heels. Her hair was dark and medium long. Her makeup was understated, except around the eyes where there was a lot of bluish shadow. Her figure was good. Her nail polish matched her lipstick. She wore a very large diamond ring and a wedding band encrusted with diamonds. She served coffee in small cups on a red lacquered Japanese tray. The cups were decorated with Japanese landscape art.

"Most of my cups have advertising slogans on them," I said.

She smiled.

"You must be single," she said.

She was sitting very straight on the forward edge of the sofa with her legs crossed and her hands folded in her lap. The coffee was on a low table in front of her. I liked her knees.

"Sort of," I said. "I'm with Susan, ah, Hirsch. But I buy my own cups."

"Susan Hirsch? Brad's first wife?"

"Uh huh."

"Is that how you know Brad."

"I suppose it is," I said. "He was facing a lawsuit and Susan asked me to help him out."

"You're not an attorney?"

I had told her on the phone that I was a detective.

"No," I said.

"What sort of trouble is Brad in now?" she said.

"Well, the ah, precipitating occasion was a lawsuit alleging sexual harassment."

Nancy Ginsberg smiled and shook her head. "Why am I not surprised," she said.

"He have a history of sexual harassment?" I said.

"No, not really. He's just so unaware. He probably doesn't know what sexual harassment is."

"Have you seen him recently?" I said.

"No."

"Do you and he get along?"

"Oh we get along. He's my big brother and I have always had a kid-sister crush on him. But . . ."

"But?"

"Well, we've had to sort of cut him off," she said. "Joel likes him. Everybody likes him . . ."

"Joel is your husband?"

"Yes."

"And everybody likes Brad, but . . . ?"

"But nobody can afford him. He always needs money. We gave him money, thinking maybe if we bailed him out once . . ." She shook her head. "Finally we had to say no."

"How did Brad take it?"

"It was awful. Brad pleaded with Joel . . ." She paused, thinking about the scene. "But we've got three kids to educate," she said. "We had to say no more."

"When was this?"

"Oh last year sometime, maybe longer, maybe a year and a half."

"And you've not seen him since?"

"No."

"Do you know why he needed the money?"

"Well, alimony, I know; and child support."

"Doesn't his business do well?"

"He always says it is. But then when he wants to borrow money he will say the money is in some bank in a foreign country and he can't get it out, or all his cash is tied up temporarily in some huge event he's doing and he'll pay us back as soon as the event happens."

"He ever pay you back?"

"No."

"You know where he might be now?"

"No, why, is he missing?"

"Yes."

"Well, my God, how long?"

"Several days, now," I said. "His office is closed. He's not in his apartment."

I decided not to mention that he was a suspect in a murder investigation. Apparently, she had missed the second-section story in the *Globe*, or the twenty-second Action News brief on Channel 3. They worried mostly about crabgrass out here.

"Do you think he's all right?" she said.

"He may have just gone off for a few days R and R," I said. "You have any idea where he might go if he wanted to get away for a while?"

"Not really," she said. "I don't know too much about Brad's personal life."

"No summer home, or ski condo or anything like that?"

"Not that I know of. Brad was always on the verge of bankruptcy," Nancy said. "I don't think he could afford anything like that."

"Know anyone named Buffy?" I said.

"Buffy Haley," she said. "Was Brad's second wife. He had two children with her."

"Know where she is now?"

"Not really. When they divorced she got the house in Winchester, but I don't know if she stayed."

"Carla Quagliozzi?"

Nancy smiled a little.

"Third wife."

"Know about her?"

"No. She wasn't around long. I think she was pregnant when they married. I don't know where she is."

"Ever hear of an organization called Civil Streets?"

"No."

"Know anyone named Jeanette Ronan?"

"No."

I tried the rest of the names in the harassment suit. No.

"Did you ever go to any of the events Brad put on?"

"No. Joel hates stuff like that. He gets home at night he wants a drink, dinner, and a ball game."

"Who wouldn't?" I said. "So you didn't attend Galapalooza, last January."

"No. I never even heard of it. Galapalooza?"

"Galapalooza," I said. "If you were Brad and you needed for whatever reason to get away, where would you go?"

She gave it some thought. I drank my coffee and admired her knees some more. The coffee wasn't very good. The knees were.

"I have no way to know where," she said. "But it would involve a woman. Brad liked . . . well, now that I start to say it, I'm not so sure . . . I was going to say he liked women. He certainly needed women. He had great luck attracting them. Have you met him?"

"Yes."

"Then you see how handsome and charming he is."

"More so even than myself," I said.

"Perhaps you're too modest," she said. "But he had a terrible time hanging on to them. Carla was, as far as I know, his last marriage, but there are certainly a lot of girlfriends. I'd look for him with a woman."

"How'd he feel about Susan?" I said.

"He always said she was the one he should have stayed with. Is the question just curiosity?"

"Probably," I said. "I'm involved because he came to her with a tale of woe. But when I spoke to him, he denied any trouble."

"You're a man," Nancy said.

"Yes, I am."

"He couldn't admit to another man that he was in trouble, or that he was anything but an All Ivy League success."

"You're saying he could get Susan to ask me to help but he couldn't admit to me that he needed help?"

"Yes."

"Wow."

"You know he changed his name?" she said.

"Yes."

"A lot of it is my father's fault," she said. "He thought that being a success in America was to join the Yankees, to be everything Brad pretends to be."

"You didn't change your name," I said.

"Well, actually, of course, I did."

"Yeah. To Ginsberg. A fine old Yankee name."

"I see your point," she said. "No, Joel and I are Jewish. We have no desire to be thought otherwise."

"So how'd you escape your father's dream," I said.

"Well, I was a girl," she said, ". . . and I got some help."

"A sound decision in both cases."

"I didn't decide to be a girl, Mr. Spenser."

"Well, I'm glad it worked out that way," I said. "You'd have been wasted as a boy."

She colored slightly and smiled.

"Well," she said. "Well, I guess, thank you."

I smiled, my low-wattage smile. I had promised Susan exclusivity, and I didn't want Nancy to fling herself into my arms.

"Anything else you can tell me about your brother?" I said.

"He's not a bad man," she said. "He's just . . . my father screwed his head up."

"You had the same father," I said, "and you did something about it."

"I know," she said.

twenty-seven

I WAS SITTING IN my office with a pad of lined yellow paper trying to find a pattern in the matter of Brad Sterling aka Silverman. Susan always said that the paper was a really ugly color, even after I had explained to her that all detectives used yellow paper with blue lines on it. It was how you knew you were a detective. But even though I was using the correct paper, I was getting nowhere, and slowly, which was another way to know you were a detective.

The phone rang. I answered.

"This is Mattie Clayman," the caller said. "From AIDS Place."

"Yes," I said. "I remember."

"I just wanted to thank you."

"I like the impulse, but what for."

"I'm used to being bullshitted," she said. "I didn't believe you when you said you'd find out what happened to our money."

"From Galapalooza," I said.

"Right."

"I haven't found out yet," I said.

"Maybe not, but you've started the ball rolling. The guy came by yesterday from the AG's office."

"What guy?"

"Guy from the Public Charities Division, said he was looking into funds distribution from Galapalooza. I assumed you'd sent him."

"What was his name?" I said.

"Didn't say his name."

"What did he look like?" I said.

"Look like? Hell, I don't know. Tall guy, sort of thin. Real good clothes. You know him?"

"I might," I said. "What'd you tell him."

"Same thing I told you."

"What'd he say?"

"Nothing really, just listened, thanked me for my time. I figured you had something to do with him showing up."

"Maybe I did," I said.

When Mattie Clayman hung up, I called the AG's office and asked for Public Charities. It took a little while, but they had no record of anybody from their office going to see anyone at AIDS Place.

"You're sure?" I said.

There was a pause while the woman on the phone thought about being sure.

"We are a government agency," she said finally.

"Which means you are not sure of anything," I said.

"Maybe."

After she was off the phone I sat for a while and looked at my yellow pad. There were probably fifty thousand tall thin guys with good clothes in the metropolitan area. On the other hand, one of them was, in fact, Richard Gavin. The phone was working for me, even better than the yellow pad. I picked it up again and dialed Rita Fiore. May as well go with the hot hand.

"What do you know about Richard Gavin," I said when Rita answered.

"Just a minute," she said. "What about Hi-Rita-how-ya-doin'-beautiful-let's-have-a-drink-real-soon?"

"That too," I said. "What about Gavin?"

"Got his own firm. It says Gavin and somebody, but it's just him. Partner went a long time ago. I guess he liked the name."

"And?"

"And what do you want to know? He's primarily criminal law. His reputation is not very good."

"Not very good why?" I said. "Competence or honesty?"

"The latter," Rita said. "He's a very clever lawyer."

"Know any of his clients?"

"Not currently. When I was a prosecutor, he used to represent a lot of mob people on the South Shore. Now I am a mainstream corporate type. Yesterday I found myself looking at a Brooks Brothers catalog for women."

"Maybe Hawk and I should come over for an intervention."

"You're too faithful," she said. "But Hawk can come over and intervene anytime he wants."

"This guy Gavin got anything to do with Francis Ronan?" I said.

"Nothing I know about," Rita said. "I mean, he may have argued a case before him. Most of us have if we do a lot of trial work."

"You know him personally?"

"To say hello. I've never been out with him."

"Puts him in a select group," I said.

"Yeah," Rita said, "you and him."

"That's only because I'm taken," I said.

"Small consolation," Rita said. "How is the thing going with Ronan?"

"Slowly," I said.

"Didn't I read someplace that they found a dead person in Brad Whatsis' office?"

"Yes."

"Things do get vexious, don't they?"

"Rita," I said, "you have no idea."

"Tell me about it over a drink," she said.

"Where?"

"Boston Harbor Hotel. It's an easy walk for me."

"Five o'clock," I said.

I hung up and called Quirk.

"You find Sterling yet?"

"No we haven't," Quirk said. "But thanks for asking."

"You got an identification on the body in the office?" I said.

"Name's Cony Brown. Long record in Rhode Island: mostly assault and extortion. Been charged twice in Rhode Island with murder, no convictions. Indicted and tried here in 1994 for assault. Case dismissed."

"Let me guess," I said. "The witnesses didn't show up."

"Close enough," Quirk said. "The plaintiff recanted."

"Who was the plaintiff?"

"Insurance broker named Rentzel, since deceased."

"Natural causes?"

"Heart attack."

"What's Providence say about Cony?"

"A shooter," Quirk said. "Freelance. Gets along with the Italians, but basically a contract guy."

"Any regular connection up here?"

"Nobody knows one."

"You didn't come across a blue disk anywhere in the office, did you?"

"What do you know about a blue disk?"

"Same thing you do," I said. "It was mentioned on Sterling's hard disk."

"How'd you happen to come into possession of information from Sterling's computer?" Quirk said.

"I forgot."

"Sometimes maybe you get too cute," Quirk said.

"What do you mean 'maybe'?"

"And sometimes maybe you do it too often," Quirk said.

"Are you keeping track?"

"Yeah," Quirk said. "I am."

He hung up without saying if he'd found the blue disk.

twenty-eight

I WAS HAVING very little success following the Galapalooza trail. Which was why I decided to revisit sexual harassment. Which is why I was sitting at my desk, studying the several nude pictures of Jeanette Ronan that I'd taken from Sterling's apartment, looking for clues. The fact that there were no clues didn't make looking a waste of time.

The existence of the pictures was a clue; so was the existence of the letters. Both raised a serious question about the validity of a sexual harassment charge. You could certainly harass someone with whom you'd been intimate. But the pictures, and the letters, some dated after the alleged harassment, would make it hard as hell to win a court case. Even if the complaint were legitimate, a lot of women wouldn't want to take it to court and have the pictures and the letters surface. Jeanette knew about the pictures. Did she really think he wouldn't keep them? Or did she have some reason to believe he wouldn't use them? Why wouldn't he use them? One good approach would be to ask her. I got the phone and called her number. She answered.

I said my name. She hung up. Maybe another approach would be good.

I looked into my case file on Sterling and found Olivia Hanson's number. I dialed. She answered.

"Spenser," I said, "with a rain check for lunch."

"The detective," she said.

"That's me," I said.

"With the short gun."

"But effective," I said. "How about that lunch now?"

She was silent for a moment.

"I won't ask you a single question about Jeanette Ronan," I said. "Or Brad Sterling."

She was still silent.

"Someplace you've been dying to go," I said.

"I don't know," she said.

"What are your plans for today?" I said. "Add a cup of hot water to some instant soup mix? Chicken noodle maybe? Watch some daytime TV?"

"You have a point," she said.

"Time to get out of the house," I said.

"Okay. But no talking about the case."

"Not a single question," I said.

"Will you pick me up?"

"Absolutely. When may I come?"

"I have to decide what to wear," she said. "And my hair . . . Come at noon."

"I'll be there," I said.

We had lunch in a place called Weylu's. It was on a hill off Route 1 in Saugus, overlooking a parking lot for school buses. The place looked like a Disney version of the Forbidden City. There was a small stream coursing through one of the dining rooms with a little bridge over it. The food wasn't bad, but given her choice of lunch anywhere she wanted, Weylu's seemed a modest aspiration on Olivia's part. Maybe Jeanette's circle wasn't as sophisticated as I'd been led to believe.

The waiter inquired as to cocktails. I ordered a Changsho beer to be authentic. Olivia had a glass of Cordon.

"So," Olivia said. "What's the best part about being a detective."

"Legitimizes nosiness," I said.

"And you get paid for it."

"Sometimes."

"How did you come to be a detective?"

She was through her first glass of wine already. The waiter was alert. He brought her another.

"I started out as a cop," I said.

"And why did you leave that?"

"I got fired," I said. "I had a problem with authority."

"Had?"

"I'm older now," I said.

She was leaning forward, her eyes on me, her whole person focused on me. It was flattering, but it was technical. It's what she did to be charming.

"Would you go back?"

"No."

She smiled as if she'd discovered the innermost me.

"Did you get your nose broken in the line of duty?" she said.

"Among other things," I said.

"Like what?"

"I used to box."

"Oh my," she said.

We ordered more food than we could eat, and Olivia had another glass of wine.

"I promised not to ask you any questions about Jeanette Ronan," I said.

"That's right," Olivia said.

She had a little trouble with the *t*'s.

"But I would like you to give her a message from me."

"How come you don' give't to her yourself?"

She wasn't doing so well with adjacent vowel sounds either.

"She won't take my calls," I said.

She drank some more wine.

"Why don' you go out there in person?"

"I don't want her husband to know," I said.

"Why not?"

"There's something involved here that he shouldn't know. I'm trying to spare her."

A pu-pu platter had arrived and Olivia sampled a spare rib while she thought this through.

"Wha's the message?"

"It's a question," I said. "I'll write it on the back of my business card."

I took out a card and wrote: *Do you have a remote control device on your Polaroid?* I handed it to Olivia who looked at it and frowned.

"Wha's this mean."

She had solved the problem with her *t*'s by dropping them.

"Nothing you should know," I said. "But it will mean something to her. And, hopefully, if it should fall into her husband's hands, it won't mean much to him."

I could see that she liked the conspiratorial overtones. *Fall into her husband's hands* pleased her.

"Okay," she said. "I'll do it."

The purpose of the lunch was over, but I felt I owed

her the full treatment, so I stayed on with her through several more glasses of wine, and increasingly flirtatious small talk. When I finally got her home, she was quite drunk. Much too drunk to conceal her disappointment when I said I wouldn't stay. I felt kind of bad about that, but I guess it was better than having her eager to get rid of me.

"Will you call again?" she said.

"Absolutely," I said.

"Being divorced sucks," she said.

"I've heard."

"Nothing out there but jerks."

"Heard that too."

"I had a nice time," she said.

"Me too," I said. "I'll call."

She put her arms around my neck and stood on tiptoe and gave me a hard open mouth kiss. I did the best I could with it. It would have been ungentlemanly not to respond. Driving back to Boston over the bridge I felt like I may have been guilty of some kind of molestation myself. I decided that when this was over, I'd take her to lunch again. The decision made me feel better. But not a lot.

twenty-nine

SUSAN CAME OVER to my place and Pearl came with her. I had promised to make steak salad and biscuits, and Pearl had apparently got wind of it. She gave me several wet kisses, then raced around my apartment nosing in every place that it was possible to conceal a steak salad. Finally she gave up and hopped onto the couch and turned around three times and lay down.

"Now it's your turn," I said to Susan.

"Do you mind if I don't sniff behind the bookcase?" she said.

I settled for the several kisses. When that was done, Susan sat on one of the stools at my kitchen counter and poured half a glass of Merlot. She had come from work so she looked very professional in a tan suit.

"We haven't had steak salad in a long time," she said.

"Well," I said, "call me crazy, but I tire of tofu."

"Fickle," she said.

I was drinking a bottle of beer.

"I like this Merlot," Susan said.

"It's Meridien," I said. "When we were in Santa Barbara we used to look at its vineyards from the top of that hill we used to run."

The steak was grilling. I was cutting mushrooms and sweet peppers and celery and scallions with a large knife on a white Fiberglas cutting board.

"In some ways that was the hardest time we've ever had," Susan said, "Santa Barbara and all that went with it. But I kind of miss it."

I turned the steaks on the grill with some tongs.

"I was pretty dependent on you when we first got out there," I said.

"Well, of course you were," Susan said. "You'd been shot and nearly died."

"That does increase dependency, I suppose."

There was a lot of activity on my couch. Pearl was rooting the pillows around trying for a better lie. She finally found one that satisfied her and she settled into it with a sigh.

Susan got up from the counter, took her wine glass, walked to the front windows in the living room, and looked down at Marlborough Street. During the fall last year, when fresh corn was a glut on the table, I had wrapped and frozen any ears left over during the time of plenty. Now that fresh corn would be more valuable than ambergris, I couldn't wait to take out a couple of frozen ears and use them. They weren't good as corn on the cob, but thawed and cut from the cob, the kernels were a lot better than the perfect and nearly tasteless ones they sell in the store. I picked up one of the ears I'd defrosted and began to cut the kernels off.

"Magnolias are out," Susan said from the window.

"Every year," I said.

I scraped the cut corn into a small bowl, sprinkled it

with very little sugar and some chopped cilantro, and put it aside.

"I wonder if my fondness for Santa Barbara might have had something to do with your dependence," Susan said.

"Well, I was sure at my least," I said.

"Physically," Susan said. "You were, and that maybe is what I'm responding to now. But in some ways you were more you than you've ever been."

"I think this may be my moment," I said. "I understand what you said."

Still carrying her wine glass, she turned away from the window and came back to the counter and sat again.

"Do you know why I've been so bitchy lately?"

"Is bitchy an acceptable phrase for a feminist?" I said.

"No. Do you know?"

"Has something to do with Brad Sterling."

"Do you have a theory on what the something is?"

"Well, I'd say something about him, or my connection to him, scares you."

"Yes," Susan said. "I think that's right. Do you know what it is?"

"No."

"That's the thing," Susan said. "I don't either, and being scared and not knowing of what makes me frantic."

"You're not used to it," I said.

"No I'm not. And," she shook her head, —"physician heal thyself—I decided simply to deny it."

"And yet you would ask about him."

"Of course, how could I not be interested? I had gotten myself into a situation I couldn't tolerate."

"And therefore . . ."

"And therefore bitchy," Susan said.

"Like you are about Russell Costigan," I said.

Susan took in a deep breath and let it out. I was finished tearing the romaine and the steaks were done. I took the steaks off the grill and put them on the cutting board to rest.

"You are so much fun," Susan said. "And you're so nice to people who need being nice to, and you're so nice to me that it is easy to forget how hard you are."

I got out a container of cajun spice that a guy had sent me from Louisiana and sprinkled some on the steaks. There was nothing to be gained here by opening my mouth.

"But it's not meanness, is it," Susan said. I wasn't entirely sure she was talking just to me. "You think I need to make the connection between how I feel about Brad and how I feel about Russell Costigan."

I nodded.

"And you know how difficult this is for me, which is why you are being very quiet."

I nodded.

"You are, of course, right, you bastard."

"Don't you hate when that happens," I said.

Susan nodded. I began to cut the steaks into small squares. Susan was quiet. I looked up at her and there were tears running down her face.

"Jesus Christ," I said.

She turned her head away. But she couldn't stop her shoulders from shaking. Pearl raised her head from the couch and looked at Susan with a mixture of annoyance and anxiety. I came around the counter and started to put an arm around her shoulder. She stood and turned half away from me. Her shoulders were shaking hard now and she was cursing to herself.

"Goddamn it," she said. "Goddamn it, goddamn it."

I moved around so I was facing her and put my arms around her. It was like embracing a coat hanger. I didn't force it. But I didn't take my arms away.

"What is wrong with me?" she said. "What in hell is wrong with me?"

"Don't know yet," I said. "But we'll find out."

And then it broke and she leaned in against me and put both her arms as far around me as she could reach and sobbed. Pearl got off the couch and came over and tried to get her head in between our thighs and failing that put her head against mine and looked up at me.

She'd have to wait.

thirty

W E DIDN'T GET to sleep until very late that night and got up far too early in the morning. Susan was very late, so she left Pearl with me for further spoiling. I fed Pearl and walked her and now she was in the office with me looking out my window and barking at things on Berkeley Street. I was drinking coffee and sharing an oatmeal scone with Pearl and trying to feel perkier when Quirk came in. Pearl abandoned me at once and hustled over. Quirk bent down low enough for Pearl to give him a lap, and scratched her behind the right ear for a moment before he straightened up.

"You got custody this week?" he said.

"It's take your dog to work day," I said. "You want some coffee?"

"Of course."

I got a cup from the storage cabinet and handed it to him and pointed at the Mr. Coffee machine on the side table.

"There's milk in the little refrigerator," I said.

Quirk poured some coffee, and added milk and

sugar. Pearl paid close attention. There was a canister of dog biscuits beside the coffee maker. Quirk took one out and gave it to Pearl. Then he came and sat in one of my conference chairs. Pearl sat on the floor beside him and put her head on his thigh.

"Why you," Quirk said to Pearl, "why not my old lady?"

Pearl wagged her tail.

"Going through Sterling's address file, we came across the name Richard Gavin," Quirk said.

I nodded.

"When we talked the other night in Sterling's office," Quirk said to me, "you mentioned a guy named Gavin who kept popping up in whatever it is you think you're doing."

"Investigating," I said. "I'm investigating."

"Sure you are," Quirk said. "Gavin has popped up again."

"And you stopped by on your way to work to share?" I said.

"Spirit of cooperation," Quirk said. "Maybe you can learn by example."

He drank some coffee.

"Good coffee," he said. "You remember the name of the stiff in Sterling's office?"

"Cony Brown," I said.

"Right. You remember he was tried for assault in Massachusetts."

"Yeah, dismissed because the plaintiff got frightened."

"Uh huh. You want to guess who his lawyer was?"

"Richard Gavin."

Quirk pointed his forefinger. "Bingo," he said.

"Richard gets around." I was thinking out loud. "He

warns me away from Carla Quagliozzi, who is Sterling's ex-wife. Number 3, I think, who is the president of a charity, of which Gavin is a board member, which was part of Galapalooza which Sterling produced. Gavin's name is in Sterling's address file . . ."

"To which you of course have no legal access," Quirk said.

"Right. And a guy who answers Gavin's description is calling on some of the other charities in Galapalooza asking how much money they made from the event."

"Is he now?" Quirk said. "You got any idea why?"

"No. All I know is that nobody made a dime, except Civil Streets."

"How much did they get?"

"I don't know," I said. "Maybe they didn't get anything either. They won't talk to me."

"I'll bet I can get them to talk to me," Quirk said.

"You have a winning way about you, Captain."

"Yeah. You want to make a wager what I'll find out?"

"If you get past the cooked books?"

"I got people can get past those," Quirk said.

"I'll bet they made a bundle."

"No bet," Quirk said.

We sat quiet for a time drinking coffee, both of us thinking.

"Here's what I know," I said to Quirk.

"See, spirit of concentration is working already."

"He talks a good game, and he puts up a nice front, and he won't admit it, but financially, Sterling is in the crapper. He's got alimony and child support. He can't pay his bills. He's apparently run out of people to borrow from. Even his sister won't lend him money."

I held up a last small corner of my oatmeal scone.

Pearl left Quirk and came over and I gave it to her. She ate it with a lot more enthusiasm than its size deserved.

"It's a mess," Quirk said. "But there's ways to get out of it. People get out of it all the time."

"Sure," I said. "The right kind of people. They change the way they manage their money. Restructure for debt relief until they get back on their feet. They might even get a better job, or pick up a night job. But Sterling's old man was a self-made success, and Sterling went to Harvard and played football and was in Hasty Pudding, and drives a Lexus and rents himself a corner office and thinks all those things are important."

"So he doesn't do the only thing that makes any sense," Quirk said. "He does something stupid."

"He does something stupid," I said. "And now he's involved with people like Cony Brown."

Quirk nodded. We both drank coffee again. Pearl lingered near my desk, in case I might eat another scone. Quirk got up and went to the side table and poured himself more coffee. He put in a careful measure of milk and two sugars. He took another dog biscuit from the canister and came over and gave it to Pearl and went back and sat down. Pearl ate the biscuit and resumed her scone watch.

"And," Quirk said, "there was Galapalooza, grossing all that dough."

"Ah yes," I said.

"So where's Gavin fit?" Quirk said.

"Don't know yet."

"And what is Gavin's connection to Carla Quagliozzi?"

"Don't know yet."

"And if you had been married to a guy and could

call yourself Carla Sterling, why would you go with Quagliozzi?"

"Might be pride in heritage," I said.

"Yeah, that's probably it," Quirk said.

"Or it might tell you how she felt about Sterling."

"And what the hell has all this got to do with the Ronan lawsuit?"

"I don't know," I said. "Got a guess?"

"Maybe nothing," Quirk said. "Maybe it's got nothing to do with it."

thirty-one

JEANETTE RONAN WANTED to meet me at ten
A.M. in the food court at the Northshore Shopping Center in Peabody. Public and anonymous. I got there
early and cruised the place to make sure I wasn't walking into a setup. She might have leveled with her husband, and the good jurist, officer of the court be
damned, was dangerous. Other than the dangers inher-
ent if you actually ate there, the food court looked safe
enough. I got a cup of coffee and sat at one of the small
tables and looked at the mall rats.

The Northshore Shopping Center had opened for
business late in 1957 with a Filene's being the first.
Since then it had divided and multiplied and roofed
over and become a vast enclosed warren indistinguish-
able from a mall in Buffalo, Boise, or San Bernardino.
It was someplace to go for young mothers with unhappy children, and old people on whom the walls had
begun to close. It provided an indoor place with security, food, bathrooms, and other people. If all else
failed, you could buy something. I was in my business
suit: running shoes, jeans, a tee shirt, leather jacket,

and accessorized with a short Smith & Wesson and some iridescent Oakley shades. I could see my reflection in the plate glass window of the bookstore opposite and I was everything the *haute monde* gum shoe was supposed to be. Maybe more.

Jeannette Ronan arrived about 10:10, which would have been right on the button for Susan, so I hadn't begun to think she was late yet. Her blonde hair was below her shoulders and gleamed of a thousand brush strokes. She wore a dark lavender suit with a short skirt, and no stockings. Her legs were very smooth and tanned the color of caramel candy. When she sat down she gave off the gentle aura of good perfume.

"Coffee?" I said.

She shook her head. Brusque. She reached into her matching purse and took out a checkbook and a big gold fountain pen.

"How much?" she said.

"To spend the night with me?" I said. "I usually get one thousand."

"Don't be coarse," she said. "How much for the photographs."

"Oh, those are free," I said. "You want the one with my body oiled, or the all-natural one?"

She spoke as if the hinges of her jaw were sore. "I will pay you for the pictures of me," she said. "How much do you want?"

She was working her tail off to be icy. But she wasn't old enough or smart enough or tough enough. She barely managed sullen.

"Jeanette," I said. "I'm not here to sell you pictures. The Polaroid stuff was just to get you here. We need to talk."

She stared at me.

"Besides, nobody will give you back blackmail items in return for a check, for heaven's sake. Next thing you'll be asking if I accept Visa or MasterCard."

She continued to stare. She held onto the checkbook and pen as if they would fend me off. Looking like she did and having money was all the defense she would ever have, if she needed one. Smart wasn't going to be part of it.

"Do you demand cash?" she said.

"No."

"Why wouldn't you take a check?"

"If I were blackmailing you, I take the check, give you the pictures, you go home and stop payment on the check. Call the cops. I try to cash it and they've got me with proof of my extortion."

"They what?" she said.

"It's okay. I'm not going to ask you for money."

"Well, how do I get the pictures?"

"You don't."

"Then . . ."

"I want information. I'm going to use the pictures to force you to give me information."

"See, you are blackmailing me."

"Yes I am. You change your mind about coffee?"

"I . . . yes," she said and her eyes shifted. "I'll have some, black."

"Fine, and if you're not here when I come back with it I will show these pictures to your husband."

"How do I know you even have the pictures?"

"There are four of them altogether," I said. "They were in with some love letters signed 'J' in a shoebox under Brad Sterling's bed."

I took one out of my jacket pocket. "Here's one of them," I said.

She looked and quickly looked away. "Put that away," she said.

Under the careful tan her face and neck flushed richly. I put the picture back in my jacket pocket.

"Large coffee?" I said.

She looked around the room. No one was paying any attention. She nodded yes to my question and I went up and got her a cup and one for me, cream, two sugars, and went back to the table with them. She had crossed her legs, which was a good thing, and was leaning back a little in her chair, being serene and ladylike in a difficult situation. I put her coffee down in front of her carefully, without spilling any, and put mine in front of me and got back in my chair. We sat. While we sat I surveyed the room. No sign of anyone intending to shoot me. Jeanette didn't touch her coffee. Susan did that too. You gave her something to eat or drink and she allowed it to sit there for a while. Maybe it was a gender thing. When presented with something ingestible, I began at once to ingest it. Jeanette met my eyes in a long look.

"Did you like what you saw in the pictures?" she said.

"Absolutely," I said. "My congratulations to your trainer."

"I'm not ashamed of my body."

"I'm not ashamed of it either."

"You said something a moment ago about spending the night," Jeanette said.

"It was an attempt at levity," I said.

"We could, you know."

"Spend the night together?" I said.

She smiled at me. It was a smile full of invitation and promise. A nice smile, very practiced.

"And all I have to do is give you the pictures?"

"It might be a night to remember," Jeanette said.

She made a small show of looking at her watch. It was gold and silver and had a big face.

"Maybe," she smiled again, "a day and night to remember."

"That a Cartier watch?" I said.

"Yes," she said, "a Panther."

"Nice," I said.

She looked at her coffee and didn't drink it.

With her eyes demurely on the coffee cup she said, "Are you interested in my offer?"

"More than the spoken word can tell," I said. "But no thank you."

She looked up and there was something like fear on her face. I knew what it was. She'd tried money and she'd tried sex. Neither had worked. There wasn't anything else.

"Well," she said, "what the fuck *do* you want?"

"I'd like you to tell me about the sexual harassment suit against Brad Sterling," I said.

"You'll have to talk with my husband," she said.

"Mm umm," I said.

"What do you mean, *'umm hmm'*?"

"I mean you want to think that through a little?"

"Why should I?" she said. "He's my husband, he's a brilliant lawyer. You'll have to talk with him."

"Does he know?" I said.

"About me and Brad?"

"Yes."

"No."

"Does he know that the lawsuit is a fraud?"

"Fraud?"

"Fraud."

"I don't know what you are talking about. I admit to a brief period of foolish sexual intimacy. But that doesn't mean he has the right to harass me."

"May I call you Jeanette?" I said.

"Of course."

She smiled when she said it. The response and the smile were automatic. Neither was appropriate to the situation.

"Jeanette," I said, "you're in a mess. And the only way out of the mess is for me to help you. But if I'm going to help you, you really have to stop trying to outwit me. I don't mean to be unkind, but you're ill equipped."

She flushed again and her eyes blurred a little as if she were going to cry.

"Here's the mess you're in," I said. "I may have a few details wrong, but I'm pretty sure about the, ah, broad outlines of it. You meet Brad Sterling while he's running Galapalooza and you're volunteering. Maybe you were interested in doing something charitable. Maybe you and your girlfriends just thought it would be fun, maybe meet some celebrities. Brad's an attractive guy, and you get involved. Then one way or another your husband gets wind of it. Maybe you love your husband, maybe you like the life he gives you, whatever, you want to save your marriage. So you say it's not what it looks like. It's a case of sexual harassment."

She was sitting very still, her coffee still undisturbed in front of her. She was trying to hold my gaze but not doing it very well. Her eyes were definitely teary.

"It's not a bad ploy. But you know who and what your husband is. And you should have guessed that he'd sue the bastard."

The tears that had blurred her eyes were beginning to spill. She picked up her napkin and blotted them, carefully, so as not to spoil the eye makeup.

"So," I said, "you got your girlfriends to help join in, make it more credible, take some of the heat off you. And your husband sues on behalf of all of you."

"He flirted with all of us," Jeanette said.

"I'm sure he did."

"So there really was some harassment," she said.

"I'm not sure flirtation's harassment," I said. "But that's not my issue."

"Well, it's an important issue," she said.

"Sure," I said. "What I don't get is why Sterling is so passive about it."

"Maybe he felt guilty," she said.

"About what?"

"Well, he was having an affair with a married woman," she said.

"Sure," I said. "That's probably it."

We were quiet. She dabbed again at her eyes. They looked fine.

"That about how it went?" I said.

She nodded.

"You wouldn't have any thoughts on where Brad might be now, would you?"

"No."

"You know he's a suspect in a murder case?" I said.

She nodded.

"See any connection between your lawsuit and the murder?" I said.

"My . . . good God no," she said. "What could that have to do with murder?"

I shrugged.

"Ripples in a pond," I said.

"Ripples?"

"Know anybody named Richard Gavin?"

"No."

"Know why your husband would hire a couple of sluggers to scare me off the case?"

"Sluggers?" She wrinkled her nose at the word. "My husband?" She was horrified. "My husband certainly wouldn't . . ."

"I'll take that as a *no*," I said. "Ever hear of an organization called Civil Streets?"

She said, "Certainly."

At last an answer.

"It's one of the beneficiary organizations for Galapalooza," she said proudly.

"Know what it does?"

"I believe it is a rehabilitating agency for criminals." She corrected herself. "Former criminals."

"Know how much they received from Galapalooza?"

"It was all pre-allotted," she said, "by share. How many tables everyone sold, that sort of thing."

"But you don't know how much they actually got."

"No."

"You know how much anyone got?" I said.

"I heard that the costs were so high that they weren't able to distribute as much to charity as they had hoped."

"I heard that too," I said.

We sat quietly. She had never touched her coffee. I had drunk all of mine and was thinking maybe she'd had the better idea.

"Anything else you can tell me?" I said.

"About what?"

"About Brad Sterling or Galapalooza or the guy got

killed in Brad Sterling's office, guy named Cony Brown, or a woman named Carla Quagliozzi or what you plan to do about the sexual harassment suit?"

"I don't know . . . What do you mean about the sexual harassment suit?"

"You can't press it," I said. "I have your letters and your pictures. You take it to court and you'll lose, quite publicly."

"But I can't tell my husband," she said in a tone that suggested that I was an idiot for suggesting otherwise.

"Well, you don't have to right now. Until we find Brad, you can probably sit tight and keep your mouth shut."

"But what if you find him?"

"If?"

"Well, maybe he won't come back," she said hopefully.

"Then the lawsuit becomes moot, doesn't it," I said. She nodded slowly. "Yes. I . . . guess . . . so."

"But take a worst-case scenario, maybe I'll find him."

She shook her head and looked at the tabletop and didn't speak.

"If," I said, "anything happens that prevents him from coming back. And if you had anything to do with it, I will tell everyone everything I know," I said.

"You don't think I . . . My God, you must think I'm simply awful."

"Yeah," I said. "I guess I do."

thirty-two

HAWK HAD BEEN bored outside of Civil Streets for nearly a week. No one had showed up there. Quirk had the accountants poking into the books, but they were having difficulty, mostly because there wasn't much in the way of books to poke into. The corporation appeared to consist entirely of some stationery and the empty store front in Stoneham Square. I wanted to know the connection between Gavin and Carla, which logically, would help explain the connection between Gavin and Sterling. Logic was less common and considerably less useful than it was cracked up to be. But it was a place to start. I could hang around Carla, and if Gavin spotted me he'd come by and terrify me again, and maybe feel, this time, he had to back it up, which wouldn't get me what I was after. It would be hard to stake Carla out covertly where she lived on the Somerville waterfront. And she showed no pressing need to drop in on Civil Streets and flaunt her presidency. The better bet was probably to follow him around, and maybe he and Carla would cross paths. If Gavin was a mob guy, he might take a little more tail-ing than if he was an account manager at Smith Barney. So I rescued Hawk from Stoneham Square.

We picked Gavin up on a rainy morning in Winthrop Square where Gavin and Warren had offices. We tracked him unseen and relentless to Starbuck's, where he had a coffee and a big bun. Then we tracked him back to Winthrop Square and stood in doorways alert for every development until about 6:45 that night when he came out and walked over to the Waterfront and went into his condo on Lewis Wharf. Hawk and I stood around for maybe half an hour more, to be sure the rain had soaked through evenly, and then we went over to the bar in the Marriott.

"Feel like a fucking haddock," Hawk said.

He ordered a Glennfidich on the rocks. I had a tall Courvoisier and soda.

"You see any clues?" I said.

Hawk looked at me without speaking. The rain had beaded brilliantly on his smooth head.

"No, me either," I said.

The bar was full of dark suits and white shirts and colorful suspenders and ripe cigars. There were a few women there, mostly in red dresses. Several were smoking cigars.

"This the best idea you got?" Hawk said.

I knew that being uncomfortable always made him peevish.

"When in doubt, follow someone around," I said.

"How come when you in doubt," Hawk said, "I get to do half the following?"

"Because you are my friend," I said.

"Oh," Hawk said. "That's good. I was thinking it was because I was an asshole."

"That too," I said.

The next morning it was still rainy, but I was better dressed for it in a brown leather trenchcoat and a Harris tweed scally cap. Hawk wore a black leather poncho and a big cowboy hat with silver conchos on the headband.

"First rule of good tracking," I said. "Remain inconspicuous."

"Exactly," Hawk said.

We stood as best we could out of the weather, drinking coffee and discussing some of our most interesting romantic encounters. Hawk's were more exotic and of a grander scale. So he got to talk more than I did. Gavin came out and walked over to Starbuck's and had coffee and a bun and walked back to his office. Hawk and I dogged his every footstep. That is, both of us dogged him on the way to. I dogged him alone on the way back, while Hawk bought us two large Guatemalan coffees and two lemon scones and caught up with me back in the doorway.

"Spot anything?" Hawk said.

"Shut up," I said.

"Shame they don't sell donuts," Hawk said.

"Pretty soon, I figure, Dunkin' will be selling scones."

"Don't it always seem to go," Hawk said.

We moved on from romantic interludes to Junior Griffey and Michael Jordan and Evander Holyfield, which turned us inevitably to Willie Mays and Oscar Robertson and Muhammad Ali, which segued into Ben Webster and June Christie, which then moved associatively to Gayle Sayers and Jim Brown, which led on to David McCullough's biography of Truman and an old Burt Lancaster western called *Ulzana's Raid*. We had started on naming our all-time all-white basketball team, which Hawk contended was an oxymoron, and had gotten as far as Jerry West and John Havlicek when Gavin came out of his office building with his collar up and got into a black Chrysler Town Car parked in front of the building with its motor running.

"Oh boy," Hawk said.

Hawk had parked on a hydrant at the right spot so that we could go whichever way Gavin could take in the one-way warren of downtown. It had denied us the comfort of a warm dry car, but we would have been warm, dry, and lonely had we done it another way.

We followed the Town Car through the maze of center city digging. Then we were on the Southeast Expressway and in time we were onto Route 3.

"This is the most excitement I had since that lemon scone," Hawk said.

The Town Car cruised at the speed limit. We lay pretty well back off of Gavin; there wasn't much traffic and the exits gave you ample warning. We were in no danger of losing him. In Hanover, they turned off and we drifted off after them and went west a few hundred suburban yards and pulled into the parking lot of an Italian restaurant named Elsie's. Gavin's driver pulled around behind the restaurant and parked. Hawk parked on the other side.

"He knows me," I said.

"I'll go in," Hawk said.

He took off the cowboy hat and the leather poncho and stepped out of the car. In two steps he was into the entryway, with barely a rain drop on his cashmere blazer. I slipped into the driver's seat in case we needed to be quick and tried to find jazz on the radio and failed. Besides all the current music, there was classical and there was a couple of music-of-your-life stations. I had long ago decided that Gogi Grant singing "The Wayward Wind" was not the music of my life, and I settled for a classical station.

In maybe two minutes Hawk came out and got in the passenger side. He was smiling.

"Richard having lunch," Hawk said.

"And you know with who," I said.

"Uh huh."

"And you are going to tell me as soon as you get through grinning like a goddamned ape," I said.

"That a racial slur?" Hawk said.

"Yes," I said.

Hawk grinned some more.

"Haskell Wechsler."

I leaned back a little in the driver's seat.

"The worst man alive," I said.

"That's Haskell," Hawk said. "Bet Gavin buys the lunch."

"Haskell know you?" I said.

"Of course."

"He spot you?"

"Of course not. Haskell don't notice nothing when he's eating."

"Let's join them," I said. "See what the specials are."

thirty-three

HASKELL WECHSLER WAS a fat guy with very little hair. What there was, he had dyed black and combed up over his baldness and plastered tight against his scalp. He had pale skin and thick lips. He wore thick glasses, a huge diamond ring on his little finger, and an assertively expensive Rolex watch on his left wrist. The collar of his white dress shirt was folded out over the lapels of his gray sharkskin suit. The top several buttons of the shirt were undone over a humongous gold chain. He had tucked his napkin into the V of the open collar. He was a niche specialist, a loan shark who belonged to no mob but found space to operate just outside the not-quite intersecting fringes of other men's power. He lent money at ten percent a week to people who couldn't possibly pay it back and squeezed them ferociously for the interest. Even when they could make the weekly vig, they never paid off the principal and remained in permanent and perilous debt to Haskell.

"Couple of bruisers at the table to the right," Hawk said as we walked in.

"If they try to shoot me," I said, "prevent them."

Hawk nodded. "I think I understand," he said and walked over and stood behind the table where the bruisers were carbo loading on linguine with clams. Gavin and Wechsler were sitting alone next to them at a table for four. I pulled out one of the empty chairs and sat down with them.

"Boy," I said, "good to see a familiar face, isn't it?"

Haskell had a mouthful of lasagna. He chewed it and swallowed and said to Gavin, "You know this guy?"

Gavin nodded. "And I don't like him," he said.

Haskell had a sloppy drink of red wine and put the glass back down and wiped his mouth on his napkin without untucking it.

"So," he said and looked straight at me, "you heard him. We don't like you. Take a fucking walk."

"I'm sure, Richie, you just give me half a chance, we could be pals again."

Without looking back, Haskell spoke to one of his bodyguards. "Buster," he said, "move this douche bag away from my table."

Buster looked like the man for the job okay, but he was in a stare-down with Hawk.

"Got another guy here, Mr. Wechsler," Buster said.

"The nigger? So move him too."

"I know the nigger," Buster said.

Something in Buster's voice got Wechsler's attention. He half turned, his fat face made fatter by the huge mouthful of lasagna he was working on. He looked at Hawk and then turned back and looked at me, then he swallowed his lasagna and wiped his mouth again with his napkin.

"Hawk," he said, mostly to himself.

"You missed a spot," I said, "over there on the right. Where the smile lines would be in a human being."

"So whaddya want?" Haskell said.

His voice had a hoarse quality as if he needed to clear his throat. And he had some kind of speech impediment, not quite a lisp, that made his *s*'s slushy.

"I want to know about Richie and you," I said, "and Carla Quagliozzi and Brad Sterling and Civil Streets, and Galapalooza and Francis Ronan and his lovely wife Jeanette, and a shooter named Cony Brown and how all of that is connected, or if it isn't, where the connections are and where they aren't."

Wechsler continued to eat as I talked. There was sauce on his shirt front and some on one sleeve of his suit jacket. His sallow face had gotten red from the energy he put into the eating. He looked at Gavin, still chewing, and said around his mouthful of food, "Who the fuck is this guy?"

"Private cop," Gavin said, "working for a loser named Brad Sterling."

"Who the fuck is Brad Sterling?"

"Nobody you know, Haskell."

"See. I don't know nothing," Wechsler said, "so take a fucking hike for yourself. Save yourself a lot of trouble, you do."

"Trouble is my middle name," I said.

"I never knew your middle name," Hawk said.

"So now you do."

"You have no obligation to converse with these men in any way," Gavin said to Wechsler. "My advice is to say nothing further to him."

"Are you Haskell's attorney?" I said.

"We'll have no further comment," Gavin said.

"How about the check," I said. "Who's going to pick up the tab?"

Gavin shook his head. I picked up a spoon and held it like a microphone toward Haskell.

"How about you, sir? Do you have any comment about the check."

"I got one comment for you, asshole. You just got yourself in serious trouble. Maybe not now, this ain't the time or place. But there will be a time and place, and you can fucking count on that."

"Just why am I in trouble?" I said.

" 'Cause you fucking bothering me at lunch is why," Wechsler said.

Gavin gestured at the waiter, who was standing around uneasily. Nothing had happened to require calling the cops, but something was in the air, and he knew it. He came promptly with the check, and Gavin gave him a credit card and he scooted away.

"You don't even read the fucking check?" Wechsler said. "How you know they ain't cheating your ass."

Gavin shrugged and kept his eyes on the waiter, who returned very promptly with a credit card slip for Gavin to sign. Gavin signed the slip, added a tip, took his copy, and stood.

"Come on, Haskell," he said and he started out. Wechsler wiped up the last of his lasagna with some bread, stuffed the bread in his mouth, and stood up chewing.

"We'll be in touch, asshole," Wechsler said and waddled after Gavin. The two bruisers stood and followed their boss. Buster studied my face as he went by. It was the first time Buster had stopped looking at Hawk. When they left, Hawk sat down beside me at the table they'd departed.

"Well, you got their attention," Hawk said.

" 'Bout all," I said.

"Looks to me like Gavin is Haskell's lawyer."

"Yes," I said.

"That's something."

"I'm not sure it's worth dying for," I said.

"Most things aren't," Hawk said. "Why we don't do it more often."

"Yeah, well, let's try not to do it this time," I said.

thirty-four

S USAN AND I were leaning on the railing of the little bridge that spanned the swan boat pond in the Public Garden, on a handsome spring day with the sun out and only a small breeze blowing. We were watching somebody's spaniel which had jumped into the pond and outraged a squadron of ducks. The ducks paddled rapidly away from him under the bridge. The spaniel didn't care. He liked it in the pond and swam around with his mouth open, looking often and happily at his owner.

"Have you any hint yet where Brad might be?" Susan said.

"No," I said. "You?"

"How would I know anything?" Susan said.

"The question was idle," I said.

"If I knew something, wouldn't I tell you at once?" she said.

"Of course," I said. "And vice versa."

She thought about that for a moment and nodded. "Yes," she said, "of course. My question was idle too."

The spaniel swam vigorously about in the pond, his

owner standing right at the edge in case the dog needed help. Occasionally the dog would lap a little of the water. The ducks had apparently forgotten about him. They clustered about one of the swan boats on the other side of the bridge luring peanuts from the passengers. A stumble bum wandered by us wearing all the clothes he owned, muttering to himself as he went. Below us the spaniel finally had enough of the pool, swam to the side, and bounced up out of the pond. His owner took a quick step back out of harm's way just before the spaniel shook himself spasmodically. Then he bent down and attached a leash to the spaniels' collar and said something to him, and they went off toward Beacon Street together.

"You fooled me," Susan said suddenly.

"Which time," I said.

"When I met you. I thought you were rough and dangerous."

"And I'm not?"

"No you are. But I thought that's all you were."

I turned and looked at her. She was staring straight ahead. "You've been talking to someone," I said.

"I called Dr. Hilliard."

"The San Francisco shrink," I said.

"Yes."

I nodded, although she couldn't see me, since she was staring intently at the middle distance. She didn't say anything. I had nothing to say. We were quiet. The swan boat came under the bridge with its attendant ducks. The first three rows of benches were occupied by a group of Japanese tourists. Most of them had cameras. I always assumed that somebody in their passport office told them that if you travel in a foreign land, and you are Japanese, you are expected to carry a camera.

"She reminded me of some of the issues we had to resolve when I went away from you before," Susan said.

"Um hmm," I said.

"My attraction to inappropriate men, for instance."

Her voice had a musing sound to it, as if she weren't exactly talking to me.

"Um hmm."

"And I said to her, 'Remind me again, if I had this need how did I end up with Spenser?' "

"You thought I was inappropriate," I said.

She turned her gaze away from the middle distance and onto me. She seemed startled. "Yes," she said.

"And now you don't," I said.

"You are the best man I've ever known. If anything, I may not deserve you."

I didn't know what to do with that, but the conversation was going my way and I didn't want it to stop.

"Because the way your father was," I said.

"And the way my mother made me feel about it."

"Your first love was an inappropriate man."

"And my mother convinced me that I didn't deserve him."

"You only deserve men like Brad, or Russell Costigan."

"Yes."

"But when you get them, you can't stay with them because they aren't up to you."

Susan smiled tiredly.

"Something like that, though I wonder, sometimes, if there's anyone who wouldn't be up to me." She said it in a way that put quotation marks around "up to me" and boldfaced "me."

"This is about why you asked me to help Brad Sterling." I said.

"I guess it is."

"So why did you?"

"Some sort of guilt, I guess. I married him for his failings and when they persisted, I left him."

"Doesn't seem fair, does it?"

In view from every place on the little bridge were flowers in spring luxuriance. On the Arlington Street side were beds of tulips which would dazzle you if you were a flower kind of guy. The ornamental trees were in lacy blossom as well, their flowers much less assertive than the tulips. There were a lot of other flowers as well, but I didn't know what they were. I wasn't a flower kind of guy.

"Brad's only fault," Susan said in a voice that seemed to come from somewhere far off, "was to continue to be what I married him for being."

I waited. Susan sounded like she might be through, but I didn't want to say anything to keep her from going on. We were quiet. The small wind moved through the flowering trees and shook some of the blossoms loose and scattered them on the surface of the pond. A brown duck with a bottle green head went rapidly over to investigate, found it not to his liking, and veered away. Susan remained still looking at the pond. She was through.

"A number of other people have left him," I said. "Including his own sister."

"I know," she said and started looking at the distance again. "Poor guy, he's lost so much in his life. Maybe . . ."

She shook her head and stopped talking again.

"Maybe if you'd stayed, he would have turned into

something else?" I said. "That's some power you've got there, toots."

"I know, I know. But . . . he very much didn't want the divorce."

"Of course he didn't. But you can't stay with someone because they want you to."

"I know," Susan said.

She knew it was true, but she didn't believe it. I took in some air and let it out.

"You made a mistake marrying Brad," I said. "And you corrected it. You took up with me for the wrong reasons and then found out they were wrong and made a mistake with Russell Costigan and corrected that. It may have been bad for them, but it was good for me and, I think, for you. There's no reason for guilt."

"And now I've got you involved in a big mess," she said.

That seemed a separate issue to me, but I thought it wise not to be picky.

"Big Mess is my middle name," I said.

She paid no attention, or if she did she was not amused.

"What kind of person acts like that?" she said.

I thought about looking at the distance for a while. But that didn't seem productive. I took in more air and let it out again, even more slowly than last time.

"A person like you or me, an imperfect person, hence human, like you or me. I have nearly all my life tended to solve problems by whacking someone in the mouth. I contain that tendency better than I used to, but it hasn't gone away. I have killed people and may again. I haven't taken pleasure in it, but in most cases it hasn't bothered me all that much either. Mostly it seemed like the thing to do at the time. But the capacity to kill someone and not feel too bad is not one that is universally admired."

"Your point?"

"You said I was the finest man you ever knew. Probably am. Most of humanity isn't all that god-damned fine to begin with. I am flawed. You are flawed. But we are not flawed beyond the allowable limit. And our affection for each other is not flawed at all."

She had stopped looking at the distance and was looking, for the first time, at me.

"And every day I have loved you," I said, "has been a privilege."

She kept looking at me and then soundlessly and without warning she turned from the bridge railing and pressed her face against my chest. She didn't make a sound. Her hands hung by her side. I put my arms around her carefully. She didn't move. We stood that way for a time as the pedestrians on the bridge moved spectrally past us. After a while, Susan put her arms around my waist and tightened them. And we stood that way for a time. Finally she spoke into my chest, her voice muffled.

"Thank you," she said.

"You're welcome."

And we stood some more and didn't say anything else.

thirty-five

QUIRK CALLED ME and asked me to come in for a talk. The thing that was unusual about it was that he asked. My office was a two block walk up Berkeley Street from Police Headquarters and I was there in Quirk's office at the back of the homicide squad room in about five minutes.

"Close the door," he said.

I did.

"Civil Streets is a dead end," Quirk said when I sat down. "We went up there last week with the Stoneham cops and tossed the office. There's nothing there. No books. No computer. No paper. Nothing at all."

"So they cleaned it out," I said.

"Maybe," Quirk said. "Or maybe there never was anything there. We talked to the building owner. He said it was rented for a year by Carla Quagliozzi, paid on time every month with her personal check. I think it was just an address."

"That's what it looked like the day I went there," I said.

"So we figured we better talk to the president, and

day before yesterday Lee Farrell called Carla Quagliozzi and asked her to come down with her attorney,"
Quirk said. "She was due here at ten in the morning.
She didn't show. Farrell called. No answer. He called
couple more times. Nothing. This morning we called
Somerville and asked them to send a cruiser by. The
cruiser guy found the front door ajar. He yelled. Nobody answered, so he opened it and looked in. She was
in the living room. Somebody had shot her in the head,
and cut her tongue out."

"Jesus Christ."

"Medical examiner says it was probably done in
that order."

"I hope so."

"ME was pretty sure," Quirk said. "No evidence
that any of the kitchen knives were used, assumption is
that he brought his knife with him."

"Hasn't this gotten ugly real quick," I said.

"It has."

"Did you, ah, find the tongue."

"No."

"So he took it with him," I said.

"That's our assumption," Quirk said. "He had to
carry the tongue away in something. It would be kind
of messy to stick it in your pocket. There's no sign that
he got a Baggie or Saran Wrap or whatever from the
kitchen, though it's possible. Assumption is he came
prepared."

"He knew ahead of time he was going to cut out her
tongue and take it away," I said.

"That's our guess."

"I hate talking about this," I said.

Quirk said, "I know."

"So, why would he take the tongue with him?" I said.

"Got a guess?"

"He was going to show it to somebody."

Quirk nodded. "As a warning," he said.

"Which is probably why she was killed."

"To shut her up," Quirk said.

"And to shut other people up," I said. "No need to cut her tongue out to keep her quiet."

"And they left the door open," Quirk said.

"Because they wanted her to be found soon."

"Before we got to anyone else," Quirk said.

We thought about it for a minute.

"But you'd figure the tongue"—Quirk made a face—"would work pretty well as a warning."

"If they could show it to everyone they wanted to shut up," I said.

"So maybe there's more than one," Quirk said. "Maybe they left the door open to be sure we'd find her and word would get out and people they couldn't show the tongue to would hear about it, and know what it meant."

"Somebody they couldn't find," I said. "Somebody missing."

Quirk sat back in his chair, his thick hands folded in front of his chin, the thumbs resting in the hollow under his lower lip.

"Like your client," he said after a time.

"Just like my client," I said.

"Who is Susan's ex-husband," Quirk said.

"Well put," I said. "No wonder you made captain."

Quirk tapped his thumbs gently against his chin. He looked at me silently, shaking his head slowly.

"So you figure her death was at least partly to be a warning to Brad Sterling?"

"Maybe," I said.

"All because somebody might have scammed some money from a charity bash?"

"Maybe."

"And they might have cut out her tongue to drive the point home," Quirk said, "but there'd be no need to take it away to show it to Sterling if they didn't know where he was."

"This is true," I said.

"So it wasn't for Sterling."

"Maybe just the fact of it, when he heard about it," I said.

"Then why take it away?"

"Good point," I said.

"So who's the tongue for?" Quirk said.

"Here's what I know," I said. "Carla is formerly married to Brad Sterling. I'm not sure which wife, but after Susan, who was the first. She is connected to Richard Gavin, who was a director of Civil Streets, who was also Cony Brown's lawyer, and Cony was killed in Sterling's office."

"You're thinking out loud," Quirk said, "and it's not a pretty sight. Tell me something I don't know."

"Couple days ago Hawk and I saw Gavin having lunch with Haskell Wechsler."

Quirk's head lifted slightly and he let his chair come forward so that his feet touched the ground. For Quirk that was a reaction approaching hysteria.

"Haskell the rascal," he said. "He spot you?"

"I sat down with them," I said.

"You would," Quirk said.

"They weren't pleased."

"They wouldn't be."

"Haskell said I was going to be tended to later."

"Haskell would mean that," Quirk said.

"If he can," I said.

"Anyone can kill anyone," Quirk said.

"I know that's true," I said. "But if I'm going to do what I do, I have to act like it's not so."

"You've gotten this far," Quirk said. "What's the relationship?"

"I don't know," I said. "Gavin acted as if he were Haskell's lawyer."

"He'd do that anyway," Quirk said. "Makes it a privileged relationship."

"Haskell could have somebody's tongue cut out," I said.

"Haskell probably would have done it himself twenty years ago," Quirk said.

"He's an executive now. Had a couple of subordinates at the next table. One of them was a little shrimp with long hair. The other one was a big guy named Buster."

"Buster DeMilo. Haskell rules with an iron fist. Buster is the fist. I don't know the other one."

"So there's an ugly murder and there's a connection to Haskell Wechsler. What's the presumption."

"The presumption is that Haskell did it, and we can't prove it."

"Right you are, Captain Quirk," I said.

thirty-six

SUSAN AND I were walking up Linnaean Street holding hands. They were halfway through laying the brick walk up to the new condominium being rehabbed out of an old Victorian next to Susan's place. The bricks were being set in stone dust instead of sand, and a pile of it made a small gray pyramid next to a half-empty pallet of paving bricks. It was eleven o'clock in the evening and the site was deserted, except for two guys who stepped out of the half-built condo. One of them had a gun and he was pointing it at me. The other one was Buster DeMilo.

"Don't do anything fancy," Buster said, "or the broad gets it too."

"Susan, this is Buster," I said. "Buster, Susan."

"Stand over there, Susan," Buster said. "And stay quiet."

Susan stepped aside. Buster's associate kept the gun on me. He was a short guy with small eyes narrowly separated by a sharp nose. His hair was long and he wore an earring. The gun was a semiautomatic, nine millimeter, probably. Maybe a Colt. The short guy seemed comfortable with it.

"You got a beatin' coming," Buster said.

"No doubt," I said. "This one from Haskell?"

"Mr. Wechsler can't allow people to embarrass him like you done. Been any worse and I'da had to kill you."

"You going to do the beating?" I said.

"Yeah."

"And Needle Nose with the gun? He's here to be sure you win?"

"They tell me you're always heeled," Buster said. "Shorty does most of the shooting."

"He shoot Carla Quagliozzi?"

Buster was putting on a pair of tan leather gloves.

"We ain't here to talk, pal," he said.

Buster feinted with his right hand and brought in a pretty good left hook. I half slipped the punch and shuffled back and a little sideways. Buster was big. Bigger than I was, and he looked in shape, and he knew what he was doing. He shuffled after me in a way that told me he used to box. If he used to, then he knew I used to by the way I'd slipped his punch. Buster grinned at me.

"Done this before, ain't ya," he said.

"Both of us have."

"I can take you anyway," Buster said. "But you make too good a fight of it and Shorty will dust the broad."

He did the same feint with his right and came around with the hook again. I blocked the hook and put one of my own over his lowered right hand and banged him on the chin. It rocked him back a step. He grunted. Shorty stepped closer, looking for direction, and while he was looking, Susan picked up a brick from its pallet and, holding it in both hands, hit him on the back of the head like someone driving a fence post. Shorty went down without a sound and the gun skittered into Linnaean Street. Buster turned at the sound and I kicked him in the groin. Buster yelped and doubled over. Susan got the gun and turned it toward Shorty before Buster had fully sunk to the ground. He lay on the ground, his hands pressed in to his crotch, his knees up. Susan had the gun in both hands as I'd shown her. It was cocked.

"You sonovabitch," Susan said. "You sonovabitch."

Shorty paid no attention. He was out. Buster wasn't out but probably wished he were. I went over and took the gun from her.

"You cock it?" I said.

"No."

"He had it cocked," I said. "Amazing it didn't go off when he dropped it."

"Yes," Susan said. "That is surprising."

Her voice was perfectly even, although she was trembling slightly. As I stood beside her the trembling stilled. Her voice was calm as iron. *After great pain, a formal feeling comes.*

"Is he alive?" she said. "The one I hit."

"Probably," I said.

"Oddly, I wouldn't care if he were not," she said.

"Why don't you go in and call 911," I said. "And I'll stay here and guard the casualties."

"Certainly," Susan said.

"That was pretty good, Wonder Woman."

"Yes," she said steadily. "It was."

She turned and walked unhurriedly into her house. Shorty had rolled over onto his back and his eyes were open but unfocused. Buster was sitting up, still clutching himself.

"We might want to try this again someday," I said. "Just you and me, Buster, without any guns, or a tough Jewess to tip the odds."

Buster had nothing to say to that and we were quiet the two or three minutes it took for a Cambridge cruiser to come whooping down Linnaean Street with its siren on and the blue light flashing.

thirty-seven

A CAMBRIDGE DETECTIVE named Kearny took our statements in Susan's downstairs office. He was in the middle of it when Lee Farrell showed up. Kearny and Farrell knew each other.

"Who fought your battles before you met Susan?" Farrell said to me.

"I used to run," I said.

"You just visiting," Kearny said to Farrell, "or has Boston got an interest?"

"Boston has an interest," Farrell said. "You people got the piece that Susan took away from one of the alleged assailants?"

"Yeah, a little bang-bang named Kenneth Philchock."

"Somerville's got a homicide, woman named Carla Quagliozzi."

"Broad got her tongue cut out," Kearny said. "I heard about that."

"She got shot first. Be good to know if it was Philchock's gun."

"Call Lieutenant Harmon about that," Kearny said. "Why is Boston interested?"

"Got a case that ties in," Farrell said.

"You want to share it with me?" Kearny said.

"Call Captain Quirk about that," Farrell said. "How are you, Susan?"

"I'm fine, Lee."

"People get shaky sometimes, after the fact."

"I know, but I'm fine."

"DeMilo and whatsisname made a statement?"

"Philchock," Kearny said. "I don't know, Lee. I'm trying to get a statement from these people, you know?"

Farrell nodded.

"I'll call Central Square," he said. "Okay?" He nodded at the phone on Susan's desk.

"Of course."

"Awful polite for a cop," I said.

"But not for a homosexual," Farrell said.

"Oh yeah," I said. "I forgot."

Farrell dialed a number.

"Okay," Kearny said. "I got what happened. Either of you got a theory about why?"

Susan shook her head.

"You know either of the assailants?" Kearny said.

"No." Susan's voice was firm.

Kearny looked at me.

"You know them?"

"Nope." I didn't look at Farrell. He didn't say anything. He was busy telling somebody at Cambridge Police Headquarters who he was.

"You make a lot of enemies," he said. "Anybody mad at you?"

"Hard to imagine," I said.

"Yeah," Kearny said. "Anybody?"

"Can't think of anybody," I said.

Farrell hunched the phone in his shoulder and looked at me while he waited to be transferred to the proper department. But he still didn't say anything and I saw no reason to get too many footprints on the problem until I figured it out better than I had.

"Guys like these two don't usually assault strangers on the street for the hell of it," Kearny said.

"I know," I said. "Doesn't make any sense, does it."

"It would make a lot more sense if this was related to you nosing around in somebody's business who didn't want you nosing around in his business," Kearny said.

"It sure would," I said.

Open and earnest, a law-abiding citizen eager to help the police. Kearny looked at me like he didn't think I was so open and earnest, and maybe even like I wasn't helping the police. Cops get cynical. Farrell had gotten connected to the proper person and talked for a moment and listened for several moments and then hung up.

"I got the feeling you're not leveling with us," Kearny said.

"I'm sorry you feel that way, officer."

"Yeah, I'll bet you are. You think he's leveling, Farrell?"

"Probably not," Lee said.

"You know anything he's holding out?"

"Nope. As far as I know, he always holds something out."

"Yeah. They got a statement from the perps?"

"They wouldn't make a statement. Just yelled for their lawyer."

"He show up?"

"Uh huh. He says there will be no statement at this time."

"Who's their lawyer?" I said.

Farrell grinned at me. "Guy named Gavin," Farrell said. "Richard Gavin."

"I'm shocked," I said. "Shocked, I tell you."

"You guys want to let me in on it?" Kearny said.

"Gavin's very active in philanthropic causes," I said. "He's on the board of a prominent charity. Hard to figure him representing these two toads."

Kearny slapped his notebook shut in disgust.

"The hell he is," Kearny said. "He's a mob lawyer. For crissake he's Haskell Wechsler's lawyer. All he ever represents is toads."

"Well, maybe he does charity work to make up," I said.

"Don't shit a shitter," Kearny said. "I don't know about you, Dr. Silverman, but you and Farrell got something you're not telling me. And you're not going to. Okay. We don't do rubber hoses anymore, so I'll eat it and go write up my report and mention that I think you're concealing evidence."

He stood up.

"Any of you got anything else to tell me that you think might be useful?"

None of us spoke. Kearny shook his head.

"Okay," Kearny said, looking at Susan and me, "we'll be in touch."

He looked at Farrell.

"Thanks for the help, Boston."

Then he put his notebook into his side pocket and went out of Susan's office. Susan looked after him.

"He's right, isn't he," she said.

I shrugged. Farrell shrugged.

"I heard the big one mention somebody that you had embarrassed."

"Haskell Wechsler," I said.

"You knew this too," she said to Farrell.

"Yeah, Quirk told me."

She looked back and forth between us.

"So why didn't you tell him what you know?" Susan said.

I shrugged. Farrell shrugged.

"I know he never tells anybody anything he doesn't need to," Susan said to Farrell. "But you're a policeman yourself, Lee."

"Maybe Wechsler's a lead for the guy got killed in your—in Sterling's office," Farrell said. "Maybe he's connected to that woman, Sterling's ex-wife got killed in Somerville. Cambridge goes after him for assault and they may screw him up for us."

"Well," Susan said. "So much for interdepartmental cooperation."

"Suze," I said. "If we can get him for murder, rather than assault, he'll go away a lot surer for a lot longer. The world is a better place with him away."

"Do you know he's the one that did the murders?"

"Or ordered them," I said. "No. Unless Lee knows something I don't know, we don't know he's guilty. But it's a good guess."

"Because?"

"Because," Farrell said, "if there's something bad going on and Haskell Wechsler is connected to it . . ." He shrugged.

"Haskell is a really genuinely bad man," I said.

"So you're both willing to let these two hoodlums, who assaulted us"—Susan was frowning—"you're willing to risk letting them slide in order to maybe get this Wechsler person for something worse."

"I'd trade those two jerks for Haskell Wechsler anytime," I said.

She looked at Farrell. He nodded. Susan looked back at me and wrinkled her nose.

"Not a very fragrant business," Susan said.

"Not very fragrant at all," I said.

thirty-eight

HAWK AND I were shooting at an indoor range in Dorchester. I had three handguns, my everyday short S&W .38, the .357 I used for big game, and the Browning nine which I kept for those exciting times when five or six shots just aren't enough. Hawk had a long-barreled .44 Magnum which will, probably, bring down a crazed bull elephant. Since you rarely run into a bull elephant in Boston, I always suspected Hawk carried it for effect. We shot for an hour or so and kept score. A small group gathered to watch. Side bets were made, the bettors tending to divide along racial lines. When we got through, both of us claimed victory. Eventually we settled for a draw.

In the parking lot Hawk said, "Maybe the numbers the same but my groupings were tighter."

"Shooting with that blunderbuss, for crissake, you shouldn't even have a grouping. You ought to put one round right on top of another."

"Groupings still tighter," Hawk said.

"If we'd both been shooting at a live target, either one of us would have killed him," I said.

"Sure," Hawk said.

He didn't say anything else until we were in his Jag heading downtown on Blue Hill Avenue.

"I'd a killed him deader," Hawk said softly.

"Sure you would have," I said.

The quality of mercy is not strained. Hawk smiled to himself as we followed Blue Hill Avenue past Magazine Street.

"Haskell made a run at me last night," I said.

"Who he sent?"

"Buster and the little gunnie that was with him in the restaurant. Buster was supposed to give me a beating while the gunnie stood guard."

"Appear that they unsuccessful," Hawk said.

"Yeah," I said. "Susan whacked the gunnie with a brick."

A small muscle moved at the corner of Hawk's mouth. We drove past Melina Cass Boulevard and turned onto Mass Ave. It was late, after eleven, and as always, the city at night was different from the city in daylight. The mercury street lamps and bright traffic lights and fluorescent neon made it seem more romantic than I knew it was. And the dark sky pressing down on it made it seem smaller, safer, and more contained than I knew it was.

"She all right?" Hawk said.

"Yes."

We passed City Hospital, which sprawled farther along Albany Street every time I saw it.

"Outta line," Hawk said, "with Susan present."

"Against the rules."

"We planning on speaking with Haskell?"

"Yep."

"He got an office on Market Street," Hawk said. "In Brighton."

"I know. Lot of people got something to settle with Haskell. There's usually a lot of firepower hanging around."

"Could call Vinnie," Hawk said. " 'Cept for me, he's the best shooter in the city."

"Or maybe we can discuss this with him when he's not surrounded by the palace guard," I said.

"Which would be when?"

"Ah, there's the rub," I said.

"He must get laid," Hawk said.

"Haskell?" I said. "Who the hell would come across for Haskell."

"He got a wife?" Hawk said.

"Same answer as above," I said.

"Yeah, you probably right. Probably buys it."

"A professional woman," I said.

I nodded. We both thought about that as we passed through the South End and crossed Huntington Avenue near Symphony Hall.

"Who runs the whores in this city," I said to Hawk.

"Tony Marcus," Hawk said.

"Right. He out yet?"

"Been out a year or so," Hawk said.

"Maybe he can help us out."

"Sure," Hawk said. "He been dying to ever since you put him in jail."

"You're a brother," I said. "You'll convince him."

"I believe I helped put him in jail."

"Well, maybe."

"And as they taking him off, I believe he say I a honkie sucking mother fucker."

"I'm sure Tony didn't mean anything personal," I said.

"When you want to see him?" Hawk said.

"He still in the South End?"

"Same place," Hawk said. "Backroom of Buddy's Fox."

"I'll bet he's a night person too," I said. "Let's go see him now."

Hawk glanced at me and shook his head, and made a right turn on Boylston Street.

"Lucky I'm brave," he said.

thirty-nine

WE PARKED AT a hydrant near Buddy's Fox and went in. It was still long and narrow. There were still booths along both walls with a bar across the back. Tony Marcus still kept his office down the hall to the right of the bar past the rest rooms. There were people of several races eating ribs and brisket. The black bartender was new since the last time I'd been here. He was slope-shouldered and strong-looking with long arms and big hands. When we got close I could see that his nose was flat and the skin around his eyes was scar thickened. He had on a starched white shirt with the banded collar open and his cuffs rolled up over his forearms.

"What can I get you gentlemen," he said.

"I'd like you to go back and tell Tony that Hawk is here to see him."

"You're Hawk?" the bartender said.

"I'm Hawk."

"Who's this?" The bartender nodded at me.

"Tonto," Hawk said.

The bartender nodded without smiling.

"Sure," he said.

He went to the end of the bar, flipped up the gate, and disappeared down the hall.

"Ever eat here?" I said.

"Sure," Hawk said. "Do some nice turnip greens."

The bartender came back. Hawk unbuttoned his jacket.

"Tony says have a drink on the house. Says he'll be out in a few minutes."

"Beer," Hawk said.

I nodded. The bartender pulled two draft beers. We leaned on the bar and sipped the beer. About halfway through the beer three black men came in together and sat in a booth near the door. None of them looked at us.

"Tall skinny kid with slick hair? Came in with the other two brothers? Name is Ty-Bop Tatum. He's Tony's shooter."

"Ty-Bop?" I said.

"What happens when you got thirteen-year-old girls naming babies," Hawk said.

"Think they just happened to stop by here for a helping of hush puppies."

"Sure," Hawk said.

"Think a big white bunny hops in every Easter and leaves eggs for the kids?"

"Sure," Hawk said.

We were nearly through our beer when Tony Marcus came down the hall with his bodyguard. Some people think a huge bodyguard will discourage people. Tony's would have discouraged the Marine Corps. He barely fit through the hallway.

"That's Junior," Hawk said. "He got his own zip code."

"Junior," I said.

Hawk shrugged.

Tony didn't speak to Hawk. He looked past him at me.

"Figured it was you," he said.

The group in the front booth had turned in their seats, and Ty-Bop had stepped out of the booth and was standing beside it. He had an earring. His longish hair was pomaded and slicked back against his skull. He was never quite still as he stood there, shifting his weight slightly from one foot to another, rocking back and forth a little on his heels, drumming with his finger against his thighs.

"How ya doing?" I said.

"You both got some fucking balls," Tony said. "Coming in here."

"Balls are us," I said. "We need a favor."

"A favor? A fucking favor?"

Hawk was looking at the bodyguard. His face had a look of benign amusement.

"What you feed him, Tony? Hay?"

If the bodyguard heard Hawk, he registered nothing. Probably too busy looming. A corner of Tony's mouth moved as if he were tempted to smile. His hair was grayer than it had been when I first knew him and his neck looked softer and his jawline was a little more blurred. But he was still a handsome man, expensive-looking, and very neat in his person.

"You sent me up," Tony said.

"Shoulda been life," Hawk said. "And you out in three years."

"I ain't some fucking street thug," Tony said. "What you want?"

"You know Haskell Wechsler?" I said.

"That prick?"

"That one," I said. "You owe him anything."

"I owe him a kick in the ass, I ever get the chance," Tony said.

"Here's your chance," I said.

"I'm waiting," Tony said.

"We want to take Haskell down," I said. "We do and it leaves all his loansharking business up for grabs. Broz is too old now to care about expanding. Fast Eddie only does Asians. Leaves you and Gino."

"And the Italians," Tony said. "And the Irish guys."

"You'll know ahead of time he's going," I said. "Gives you an edge."

"Whaddya want from me?"

"Haskell's always got a lot of shooters around him."

" 'Course he does," Tony said. "Everybody knows him wants to kick his nasty ass."

"We need to get Haskell alone, and the only time we can think of," Hawk said, "is when he's getting laid."

"You think Haskell can get laid?"

"We figure he pays for it," I said.

" 'Course he does," Tony said. "Who would fuck him but a whore?"

"So you run the whore business in town."

"Yeah?"

"If he was to employ a whore," I said, "and she was to let us know where and when, and bow out, we could go talk to Haskell."

"That's the favor?"

"Uh huh."

"And when he goes down, you let me know, first. 'Fore it happens."

"Uh huh."

Tony smiled gently to himself. I could tell he liked it.

"I'm going to be thinking about it," he said.

He turned and squeezed past his bodyguard and walked back down the hall. The bodyguard followed, completely screening Tony from view. Hawk and I watched him go for a moment and then went toward the front door. The skinny shooter held his ground as we came to the door.

" 'Shappenin', Ty-Bop?" Hawk said

Ty-Bop was no more than twenty. He had light skin and small, nearly oval, black eyes. The eyes were depthless, like a snake's. He put his left fist out and Hawk bumped it with his left. Ty-Bop stepped aside and we went out into the South End.

"Good you know the language," I said to Hawk.

"Surely is," he said. "Got to take special care with the children."

We were driving up Tremont Street, past Bay Village, toward Charles Street.

"What do you think Ty-Bop's life expectancy is?" I said.

"If he don't mess with me? Tony will use him up in maybe five years."

"And I suspect he knows that," I said.

"I imagine he do," Hawk said. "Right now he gets respect."

"Because he's willing to shoot anybody at all."

"Ty-Bop ain't got much other way to get respect," Hawk said.

"I know."

We drove through Park Square and stopped for the light at Boylston. The Common sloped up to our right. The Public Garden lay flat to our left.

"Kids like Ty-Bop bother you?" I said.

"Yeah."

"Me too," I said. "You got any idea what to do about them?"

"No."

"Me either."

forty

HAWK CAME INTO my office on Wednesday morning with a young Asian woman.

"This is Velvet," Hawk said. "Tony arranged for us to talk with her."

"See," I said, "another triumph for charm and civility."

"Tony says you take Haskell out he knows ahead of everyone."

"Sure," I said. "Hello, Velvet."

"Hello."

Velvet looked maybe eighteen. She was wearing faded blue jeans and a loose white tee-shirt. Her only makeup appeared to be lipstick. She stood quietly in front of my desk.

"Sit down, Velvet," I said.

She sat.

"Would like coffee?"

"Yes, please."

"Cream and sugar?"

"Yes, please. Two sugar."

Hawk got her some from the Mr. Coffee pot. Then he sat beside her.

"Haskell got a regular contract with Velvet," Hawk said.

"Is Velvet your real name?" I said.

"No."

"What is your real name?"

"Kim Pak Soong."

"You're Korean."

"Yes."

"You're a prostitute?" I said to Velvet.

"Yes."

"Do you know who Tony Marcus is?"

"No."

I smiled. She was at the far other end of the chain of command.

"But you know Haskell Wechsler."

"Haskell. Yes."

"You have regular appointments with him."

"Yes."

"Tell me about them."

"I would not tell anyone these things, but Clifton says I must."

"Clifton's your pimp?"

"Yes."

"Where do you meet Haskell?" I said.

"Charles River Motel. He always has room 16."

"In Brighton, on Western Avenue?"

"I don't know name of street. It is near the river. Past the television station."

"How do you get there?"

"Man comes in a car, picks me up, and takes me there. When we are through, man takes me back."

"Is Haskell always in the room when you get there?"

"No. I go first, man lets me in. Then I get ready. Mr. Haskell like me to wear kimono, silk slippers, lots of makeup. Mr. Haskell comes maybe half hour after I do."

"He's alone?"

"Yes."

"How long usually?"

"He stay an hour, maybe hour and half. He doesn't fuck me all time. He brings a bottle. We drink some of it. Mr. Haskell like to talk."

"Who leaves first?"

"Mr. Haskell. After he is gone, I take shower, change clothes. Man comes back for me.

"You do this regularly."

"Tuesday and Thursday."

"So you're scheduled for tomorrow."

"Yes."

"What time?"

"Three o'clock."

I sat back in my chair and thought about things. Velvet drank her coffee.

"Clifton say you should do what we ask you to do?"

"Yes."

I looked at Hawk.

"Smart move would be to scope this all out tomorrow and make our move next Tuesday."

"Yep."

"Want to do it that way?"

"Nope."

"Tomorrow?" I said.

"Yep."

I leaned back in my chair some more, looking at Velvet.

"Okay," I said finally, "tomorrow here's what we need you to do."

Velvet listened with full attention while I told her. She seemed solely interested in doing what she was supposed to. She showed no interest at all in why.

forty-one

W HILE WE WERE having dinner at Rialto, Susan said, "We spent so much time talking to the police after the incident the other night that we haven't really discussed it with each other."

"I know it."

The waiter brought us a serving of broiled little necks.

"Hot," he said to Susan.

"Like her?" I said.

"Just like her," he said.

Susan said, "Thank you, Francis," and smiled at him enough to weaken his knees, though when he walked away he seemed stable enough. Maybe I was projecting.

"When I was alone, after it was all over, and you'd gone, I got very shaky and felt like crying."

"Post traumatic shock syndrome," I said wisely.

"That's usually somewhat more post trauma than this was," she said. "Though you are very cute to use the phrase."

"I was trying to sound smart," I said.

244   Robert B. Parker

"Settle for cute," Susan said.

"Damn," I said. "I've been settling for that all my life."

"Anyway. I didn't cry."

"Nothing wrong with crying," I said.

"I don't like to," she said.

I shrugged. Francis came by and refilled our champagne glasses.

"Regardless," I said. "You looked pretty good with that brick, little lady."

"Do you ever get shaky after something like that?"

I thought about it. "Mostly no," I said. "But I've done more of it than you have."

"Mostly no?"

"Yeah."

"But not always no?"

"Sometimes depends on the situation. Long time ago, in San Francisco, when I was looking for you, I had to shoot a pimp because if I didn't he'd have killed two whores. I had problems with that afterwards."

"Because it was cold-blooded?"

"Yes."

"Even though it was necessary?"

"More than that, it was my responsibility. Hawk and I got the whores into trouble with the guy. It was the only way to get them out."

"Did you feel like crying?"

"I threw up," I said.

"Oh," Susan said. "Did it bother Hawk?"

"No."

"Hawk's life has desensitized him in many cases," Susan said.

"But not in all cases," I said.

"Which is a triumph," Susan said.

We were quiet while we ate the clams. Susan washed her last one down with a swallow of champagne.

"I must admit," Susan said, "that I feel better about my own reaction, knowing you sometimes have one."

"You don't have to be so damned tough," I said.

"I don't wish to be stereotypically frail about things."

"Tough is what you do, more than it is how you feel about it before or after," I said. "You're tough enough."

"I haven't been so tough about my past," she said.

Francis came and cleared the clams and brought us each a salad of lobster and tiny potatoes. He topped off our champagne glasses without comment.

"You mean Sterling," I said.

"And Russell Costigan, and all of that," she said.

"You seem to me to have handled it pretty well," I said. "Here we are."

"But I have you embroiled in something bad because of it, because of . . . my former husband. That incident the other night was connected, wasn't it?"

"Probably."

"And Carla Quagliozzi?"

I shrugged.

"Did I hear something about her tongue being cut out?"

"After she had been killed," I said.

"She was one of Brad's ex-wives."

"Yes."

She shook her head.

"Things just don't go away," she said.

I ate a potato and was quiet.

"I just wanted to pretend all that never happened," she said. "But I couldn't."

I nodded and chewed my potato. It was good.

"I chose those men for their weaknesses, and then rejected them for their weaknesses."

"You said that already. No need to beat yourself up about it."

"But there's a part I haven't ever said. Not even to you."

"No need," I said.

"There is. I have caused too much trouble by not saying it."

"Long as you say it to yourself," I said.

She shook her head. "One of the reasons I was attracted to these men was that, in their imperfection, I felt safe. I knew they could never get to me."

"Get?"

"One of the aspects of my family struggle when I was little was, of course, that if my father's affection for me ever got out of hand, and my mother's worst fears were realized . . ."

"You had to keep him from getting you," I said.

"And having learned that, it got transferred to all the other men I knew."

"Including me."

"The more powerful and good and complete you turned out to be," Susan said, "the more I feared that you'd get me."

"And now."

"Now, now for crissake, I know you don't even want to get me."

"True. And if I did, you wouldn't let me."

"For which I can thank Dr. Hilliard."

"So what's that got to do with how you should have faced up?" I said.

"I got you into this because I still feel guilty about it."

"If you hadn't gotten me into this, someone would have gotten me into something."

"But it wouldn't have been me," she said.

"And you feel guilty about getting me into trouble because you felt guilty about Sterling."

"Yes."

"Well, stop it," I said.

"Stop feeling guilty?"

"Yeah."

Susan stared at me for a moment and then began to smile.

"There are people in my profession who would faint dead away to hear you say that."

"But you're not one of them," I said.

Her smile widened some more. "No," she said. "I'm not one of them."

We sat for a while in silence. Then Susan, still smiling, raised her champagne glass toward me. I raised mine and touched hers.

"Here's looking at you, Sigmund," she said.

And the laughter bubbled up out of her like a clear spring.

forty-two

Hawk and I sat in the parking lot of the Charles View Motel on Thursday afternoon waiting for Velvet to be delivered. The motel was a wooden building with pseudo redwood siding, and blue shingle roof. It stood two stories high with entrances to the rooms through individual doors facing the parking lot. A balcony across the front gave access to the second-floor rooms. It was a dark muggy day. There were thunderstorms in the area, and their tension hung undissipated in the air. At 2:30, a white Cadillac sedan pulled into the parking lot and Velvet, carrying a small overnight bag, got out one side. Buster got out the other. They went without stopping at the motel office to room number 16, last one on the first floor. Buster produced a key and opened the door. Buster went in first, after a minute he came back to the Cadillac, and drove off. I got out of Hawk's car and walked to room 16. Velvet let me in.

"See the dark green Ford Mustang, front row, parked opposite this room?"

"I do not know Must-ang."

"Green car, tan soft top right there." I pointed.

The mustang flashed its headlights.

"Yes."

"Man named Henry Cimoli is driving. He'll take you wherever you want to go."

"I want to go home."

"He'll take you there."

Velvet nodded. She picked up her overnight bag and started out the door.

"Thank you, Kim," I said.

She turned with a startled look for a moment. Then she nodded seriously and walked toward Henry's car. I watched her get in. And I watched Henry drive her away. Then I went into the motel room and closed the door.

It was the kind of place you'd bring somebody you picked up at the bowling alley. The air conditioning was noisy. The bath was tiled in plastic. The dark stain on the pine bed and bureau set was scarred. The chenille spread on the bed was frayed along the edges and thin from frequent washing. On the bureau was a bar setup: cheap bourbon, ice, a pitcher of water, a shrink-wrapped pack of plastic drinking cups. Haskell, you elegant fool!

I didn't want Haskell to see me when he opened the door, because I didn't want to have to chase him around the parking lot. I went into the bathroom and waited. It was maybe twenty minutes, but it's a long twenty standing in a small bathroom in a low-rent motel. I was wishing I had to go. It would have given me something to do. I heard the key turn in the front door. The door opened. I heard a step. The door closed. I took my gun out and held it by my side.

Haskell's voice said, "Velvet."

He sounded annoyed. But Haskell always sounded annoyed. Probably was always annoyed. I came out of the bathroom. Haskell had no reaction. He squinted at me for a moment. I stepped between him and the door. He noticed.

"Where's Velvet," he said.

"Not today."

"I know you," he said.

"Yes you do."

"What the fuck are you doing here?"

He scratched absently his chest with his right hand. He scratched a little lower on his stomach. I showed him the gun. He stopped.

"Turn around," I said. "Put your hands behind your head. Lace your fingers."

"This a fucking roust, or what?" he said as he turned.

He looked like he'd assumed the position before. I kept my gun in my right hand as I patted him down. He had a gun on his belt, left side, butt forward. I unsnapped the guard strap and took the gun off him and stepped back.

"Okay," I said. "You can turn around and put your hands down."

Haskell turned and dropped his hands. I put my own gun back on my belt.

"So what do you need," he said.

If he was scared, he was doing a masterful job of covering it. He probably wasn't scared. Being scared would have been too human for Haskell. He was probably too mean and too shallow to be scared.

The gun I'd taken from him was a cheap semiautomatic I'd never heard of. I took out the magazine, ejected a round from the chamber, dropped the gun and magazine on the floor, and kicked the gun under the bed. I was still between Haskell and the door.

"I don't know what the game is," Haskell said, "but you are getting yourself in deeper, pal."

Haskell was probably wearing different clothes than he had the last time I saw him, but he looked just the same. Haskell would always look pretty much the same.

"You broke the rules," I said.

"What rules?"

"You don't take it home," I said. "You don't involve family."

"What family?"

"Susan Silverman."

"Who the fuck is she?"

"My family," I said.

"I don't know what you're talking about."

Haskell looked momentarily at the window. It was to the right of the door as you come in, one of those fixed metal frame jobs with the air-conditioning unit on the floor under it. It wouldn't open. To go out it, you'd have to go through it.

"When Buster made his run at me," I said. "I was with Susan, outside her house."

"What the fuck do I care where you were," Haskell said.

"That's the point of my visit," I said.

"Who knew it was your girlfriend," Haskell said. "Shit happens."

"I can't let it slide," I said.

"So, whaddya want? Money? What? How much you need?"

"You have a choice," I said. "I can take it out of your hide, or you can buy me with information."

"Information? About what, for crissake?"

"What the deal was with you and Gavin and Brad Sterling."

"Sterling?"

"Uh huh."

"I don't know no fucking Sterling."

I sighed and hit Haskell in the stomach with my left hand. He gasped and stumbled back a step and bent over. As he was bending I jabbed him on the nose and straightened him back a bit. His nose started to bleed. He tried to stop the bleeding by pinching his nose and stepped back another step and sat on the bed.

"You busted my fucking nose, for crissake," he said.

"Not yet."

"I'm telling you I don't know no whatsisname Stevens."

"Sterling," I said. "Okay, tell me about you and Gavin."

"Gavin's my lawyer. You know that."

"How are you and he connected to Galapalooza?"

"To what?"

I reached over and tapped him on the nose with the back of my left hand.

He said, "Ow," and scrambled backwards on the bed to stay away from me.

"Galapalooza," I said.

"Honest to God," Haskell said, his voice thick because he was holding his nose. "I don't even know what a Lala-whatever is."

Haskell was winning this. I was okay at fighting, but I wasn't much at beating people up. I was hoping he'd fold before I'd gone as far as I could go. But he wasn't folding and I was about out of beating.

"What's the current scam?" I said. "You and Gavin?"

The blood was seeping between his fingers and staining his shirt front. He could see himself in the mirror, and I think it scared him.

"We run a little money through him," Haskell said.

"He wash it?"

"Yeah."

"How?"

"He never said. Talk to him, for crissake. I don't know what he's doing."

It made sense. Galapalooza was an excellent money-laundering vehicle. Haskell wasn't winning this. He really didn't know anything. I went into the bathroom and got a hand towel and soaked it in cold water and wrung it out and went back and handed it to Haskell.

"Okay," I said. "I'll mark your fine paid. I'll talk to Gavin. I find out you lied, I'll be back."

"I ain't lying."

"Anybody, you, someone employed by you, someone related to you, someone that knows you, comes within sight of Susan Silverman again and I'll kill you," I said.

"I don't know her. I got nothing to do with her," Haskell said.

"Keep it that way," I said. "One reason for this meeting is to help you understand that I can get to you."

Haskell was pressing the damp towel against his nose. It muffled his voice.

"Talk to Gavin," Haskell said.

forty-three

I MET RICHARD GAVIN for lunch at a steak house in Quincy Market. The weather was good and they had opened the atrium doors so that you could eat your steak and still feel connected to the ceaseless mill of people in souvenir tee shirts and plaid shorts mispronouncing Faneuil Hall and looking for a fried dough stand.

Gavin and I sat at a table next to the atrium door. A rangy guy in a tan suit stood just outside the atrium. Another guy shorter and a bit wider stood on the other side of the opening. He wore a gray suit. Both of them had on official security service sunglasses and little microphones in their lapels. I knew the rangy guy. His name was Clarke. He'd been in the Marshal Service. Now he worked for a big private security firm in town. When we sat down I shot at him with my forefinger. He nodded briefly.

"Why the bodyguards?" I said.

Gavin shook his head.

"You said you had a proposal," Gavin said. "You want to make it?"

He looked tired and the lines on either side of his mouth seemed deeper than I remembered. A waitress came and took our order.

"Actually it's more like a hypothesis," I said. "I wanted to share it with you. See what you thought."

"I don't have time for hypotheses," Gavin said. "And I have a lot less for you."

"I figure you and Sterling were in business together," I said. "With Haskell."

"I don't much care what you figure," Gavin said.

The waitress brought him a martini. I had a club soda. The martini looked good, but I had no time to take an afternoon nap.

"I figure that Sterling had money trouble. He'd run through his family, and friends, and so he did what he had done before when he was in trouble. He went to an ex-wife."

Gavin sipped his martini and looked at the menu.

"And the ex-wife he went to was Carla Quagliozzi."

Without looking up from the menu, Gavin said, "So?"

"Carla didn't have money to give him, or if she did, she was too smart to give it to him. But she was by now your girlfriend and she sent him to you. I don't know, you can fill it in later. Maybe she saw a chance to turn a profit. Maybe she felt sorry for him. His ex-wives seem to. Whatever her reason, you saw something useful. You saw a way to launder money and maybe make a profit on it in the process."

The waitress returned. Gavin ordered steak tips and another martini. I had a salad. A big lunch is nap city too. Gavin folded his menu, handed it to the waitress, leaned back in his chair, and looked straight at me.

"Why would I care about laundering cash?" he said.

"Because you're Haskell Wechsler's lawyer and he's in a cash business."

"Everyone has the right to a lawyer," Gavin said. "I'm a member of the Massachusetts Bar."

"Sure," I said.

Gavin drank the rest of his martini. The security guys were being profoundly casual just outside the steak house. The waitress brought Gavin's new martini and he rescued the olive from the old one before she took the empty glass away. She looked at me. I shook my head. Gavin ate the olive he'd rescued and put the ornamental toothpick down on the bread dish and turned it carefully so that it was nicely centered on the curve of the rim. He studied it a moment, pushed it a millimeter closer to the rim, and then sat back again.

"How exactly did I pull this off?" Gavin said. "This laundering deal with Sterling."

"I'm not sure of the details, but the general outline is like this. You or Haskell would take some of Haskell's cash and use it to fund one of Sterling's promotions. Because it was a charitable enterprise which often received cash contributions, the large cash amounts never caused a ripple. Sterling was probably exempted. The event would transpire and one of the beneficiaries would be Civil Streets, which is a dummy company that you created with Carla's name on the door. Once the money was in Civil Street's account, Carla could write checks or transfer funds to anybody she wanted. Maybe you could too and it would go back to Haskell, or another dummy company you set up for him, and his money would be washed and show a little profit to boot."

Gavin's steak sandwich arrived, nearly covered with a sumptuous mound of narrow French fries. The waitress seemed sort of contemptuous as she put my salad in front of me.

"So what went wrong?" Gavin said.

"I don't know," I said. "Maybe the sexual harassment lawsuit. It would call attention to Sterling and to Galapalooza. What I know about Sterling, he could screw up a stroll in the garden, so it may have been something else.

"Didn't Sterling invite you in?" Gavin said.

"Yes, that bothers me too," I said. "If he was involved in some kind of illegal activity, why ask a detective to look into his affairs?"

Gavin spread his hands as if to say, *there you go.*

"I'll have to splice the answer to that in later," I said. "But whatever his reasons, I was in, and either my being in, or the lawsuit, or whatever fast one Sterling had pulled, or all of the above convinced someone that action was needed. Someone, I'm guessing you, sent your old client Cony Brown over to talk to Sterling. And for reasons I haven't got yet, Sterling shot him and ran off. He took a blue computer disk with him. My guess is that the details of the money wash are on it. So he's out there like a loose cannon and you can't find him, and he has evidence that will sink you, and probably Haskell with you. And if you take Haskell down, you know that you're as good as dead. But as long as Sterling is running from the cops, he won't be talking to them. But Carla knows all this too, and she knows that Sterling is a loose cannon, and maybe the stress of it is getting to her and maybe the metal of her resolve is starting to fatigue."

I paused for a moment to admire the felicity of my metaphor. Gavin was drinking his martini. He hadn't touched his lunch.

"So you killed her. It would shut her up and it would serve as a warning to Sterling, and to make sure he got the warning, you cut out her tongue."

Gavin didn't say a word. Very slowly he put his martini glass down on the table, placing it carefully in the exact place it had been where the faint damp outline of the glass still showed. He stared at the glass.

"What I don't get is why you took her tongue with you," I said.

Gavin made no sound. Slowly at first, and then more rapidly, tears began to run down his cheeks. I could hear his breath going in and out. We sat just like that for a time that seemed very long.

"You son . . . of . . . a . . . bitch," he said finally.

He didn't seem out of breath. It was as if as he spoke he had to re-remember what he wished to say after each word.

"I . . . loved . . . her."

Then he said nothing and sat looking at his martini glass with the tears running silently down his face. I watched him for a while. The pain was genuine. I was watching grief and I'd seen enough of it to recognize it. Grief didn't mean he was innocent. He could be crying because he killed her. But I didn't think so. His hopelessness was too profound. His loss was too irredeemable. And his pain was undiluted by guilt. I didn't know I was right, but I had seen far too much of all of that as well to think I was wrong.

"I'm sorry," I said and stood up and walked out past the security men.

forty-four

MISTRAL WAS A new restaurant that had opened up on Columbus Avenue in the old Cahners building. It had a high ceiling and arched windows and the food was good. An extra plus was that it was about a three-minute walk from Police Headquarters and a five-minute walk from my office. So help was close at hand.

Hawk and I were at the bar drinking beer, eating oysters, and watching the sleek foodies.

"So we didn't take Haskell down after all," Hawk said.

"I know," I said. "Marcus will be disappointed."

"He'll get over it," Hawk said.

"And he can take satisfaction in having done the right thing."

"Sure he can," Hawk said. "Haskell not going to let you rough him up and get away with it."

I shrugged.

"He send couple of people to clean you clock for sitting down at lunch with him," Hawk said. "How you think he feel about getting hit."

"I scared him some," I said.

"Sure you did. You scary. But Haskell too mean to stay scared. We going to have to watch your back for a long while."

"Haskell will have to take a number," I said.

A tall blonde woman with a good tan walked by wearing white sling back shoes and as small a white linen dress as was legal in Massachusetts. Hawk and I watched her all across the room to make sure she wasn't one of Haskell's people. When she was seated and partly hidden by the menu she was handed, Hawk turned back to me.

"You watching my back," I said to Hawk.

"She got a weapon," Hawk said, "be hard to think where she's concealed it."

The oysters were from the Pacific Northwest and were served with a dab of citrus sorbet on top. I got a taste of the sorbet on my fork, added an oyster, and slurped it in. Excellent.

"And you buying Haskell's story," Hawk said.

"Yeah."

"Well, you done this work before, 'spose you learn who to believe."

I drank my beer. "I hope so," I said.

"So if Haskell didn't have the woman killed, who did?" Hawk said. "Gavin?"

"I don't think so," I said. "He was in shock, and he had a couple of security people with him."

"Freelance?"

"No, legit guys from that big security outfit the former commissioner works for. One of them was Kevin Clarke."

"Used to be a marshal," Hawk said.

"That's right. Anyway, when I suggested to him he

might have killed his girlfriend and cut out her tongue, he started to cry."

Hawk shrugged.

"He loved her," I said. "He wouldn't have killed her like that."

"I seen guys shoot a roomful of people and feel bad afterwards," Hawk said.

I shook my head.

"He loved her," I said.

"You the romantic in the group," Hawk said and ordered more beer and oysters.

The tall blonde woman in the minimal dress got up from her table and walked toward the ladies' room. She walked as if she were balancing a book on her head and everyone were watching to see if she could do it.

"She went to the ladies' room," Hawk said.

"Uh huh."

"Which mean she will be coming back."

"Stay alert," I said.

Hawk drank some beer and ate two oysters and patted his lips with a linen napkin.

"So it ain't Haskell and it ain't Gavin, who you got in mind for it?" Hawk said.

"Well, it could be person or persons unknown," I said.

"A perennial favorite," Hawk said.

"Or it could be Sterling."

"Wondered when you'd come 'round to him."

"I'm not happy with it," I said.

"Don't blame you," Hawk said.

"How could a guy that Susan would marry kill his ex-wife and cut out her tongue?" I said.

"Well, Susan seen something in him," Hawk said.

The white dress paraded back from the ladies' room. We watched her, listening for a flourish of trumpets. She was listening too.

"You've been talking to Rachel Wallace," I said after the blonde had sat down.

"We had a drink couple weeks back," Hawk said. "Faculty club at Taft."

I had a moment of quiet contentment as I imagined Hawk at the Taft University Faculty Club.

"And she shared her theory," I said, "that Susan is drawn to men whose faults appeal to her."

"Would explain you," Hawk said.

I drank some beer and looked out the window at the tops of city buildings arranged appealingly across the line of sight.

"You take the scenario I painted for Gavin," I said, "of why he or Haskell would want to kill Carla Quagliozzi, it would work pretty well for Sterling too, if he feared she might tell. The cut tongue could be a message to Gavin."

"But he got a secret, why does he ask you to help him with the harassment suit?"

"Because he was afraid it would shed too much light on his life and the other stuff would show."

"So why didn't he just flash the nude pictures to Jeanette Ronan's hubby?" Hawk said. "That would stop the harassment suit."

"Chivalry?"

"A dude who will kill a woman and cut out her tongue?"

I shrugged.

"You show the pictures to Judge Ronan?" Hawk said.

"Jeannette," I said.

" 'Cause you didn't want to get her in trouble," Hawk said.

"I figured she'd find a way to call it off."

"You soft hearted for a guy with no neck."

"I have a perfectly good neck," I said. "I just wear my collars high, like Tom Wolfe."

"Sure," Hawk said. "So what you going to do now?"

I shook my head.

"I have no idea," I said.

forty-five

I WAS SITTING ON a round bench with Susan in the center space of the Chestnut Hill Mall, which was swankier than Ivana Trump. There were several shopping bags around me on the floor, each of which had things in them that Susan had bought and I carried.

"Do you like that white silk jacket?" Susan said.

"Breathtaking."

"And you don't think it makes me look fat?"

"No I don't"

I had learned over the years not to give smartass answers to the kinds of dumb questions Susan asked when she shopped. It was nothing she could help, and no amount of smart talk on my part could dissuade her from it. Giving a widely amusing answer to such questions in fact tended to call forth more questions.

"You're not just saying that?"

"No."

"And the platform sneakers? Do you think they are, you know, too something."

"They look great," I said.

"Not too too?"

"Definitely not," I said. "Things look good because you wear them."

There was a live combo playing jazz in the center of the mall, which meant, I suppose, that the demographics of the mall skewed mature. Like me.

"But you don't like them only because I'm wearing them," Susan said. "You'd like them on other people."

Simple yes and no, I reminded myself. You elaborate, you get into a swamp. "They're great looking on anyone," I said. "On you they are podiatric perfection."

She was content. The combo was doing a nice job on "Sleepin Bee." We listened.

"Harold Arlen," I said.

Susan nodded as if she were interested. But I knew she wasn't. Susan didn't care whether it was Harold Arlen or Arlen Spector. The combo went into "A Foggy Day." We were alone on the bench. My hand was on her right thigh. She put her hand over mine. I took in a large breath of mall air.

"There's some reason to believe that Brad Sterling has killed two people," I said.

She was still. The music played. People moved past us carrying bags. Susan turned slowly to look at me.

"Tell me," she said.

I told her. She listened quietly. Now and then she nodded her head. When I finished she was very inward for a time. I waited. The combo moved from "Foggy Day" to an uptempo take on "Summertime."

"Well, it's logical," she said. "Though I can't imagine him doing it."

"Person or persons unknown is still an option," I said.

"But not a useful one," Susan said.

"No."

"I wonder if I overreacted when he came to me," she said. "I'm certainly capable of it, Ms. Fixit."

There was no sound of guilt in her voice. She was analytic. She could have been talking about people she barely knew.

"Someone complains to me about being over-weight," Susan said with a half smile, "I immediately suggest ten steps to solve the problem, when all they wanted was for me to say, 'You're not so fat.'"

"Probably a useful trait though, in your profession," I said.

"Actually, a more useful trait in my profession is listening quietly."

I nodded.

"Maybe all Brad wanted when he came to me was for me to say, 'Oh, poor baby.' Instead I involved you, and if you are right, it's the last thing he would have wanted."

"Or maybe he just wanted money," I said.

Susan shook her head emphatically. "I know better than to give him money," she said.

"Or maybe he was already in way over his head and was half-hoping I could save him without knowing what I was saving him from."

Susan smiled sadly. "Yes," she said. "That's exactly the kind of hare-brained scheming Brad would be capable of. Do you think you can find him?"

"I think he'll find us," I said.

"Because?"

"Because he's shown a pattern of running for help to the women he's known," I said.

"Yes, that's consistent."

"His sister has shut him off," I said. "Carla's dead.

There's at least one other ex-wife. I don't know where. But he owes her child support, and few things annoy an ex-wife more."

"So he'll come to me," Susan said.

"Sooner or later," I said.

She nodded.

"When he does," I said, "remember he may have killed two people."

Susan nodded again. She was looking straight into my eyes.

"If he appears," she said, "I will call you at once."

"Oh good," I said.

forty-six

JUDGE FRANCIS RONAN came into my office wearing a seersucker suit and a blue shirt. His yellow silk tie matched his yellow silk pocket handkerchief. You don't see that many seersucker suits anymore, and I thought that was a good thing. He sat down in one of my client chairs and crossed his left leg over his right. He wore wing-tipped cordovan shoes and blue socks with yellow triangles that matched his tie and show hankie. He was freshly shaven and smelled gently of bay rum. He rested his elbows on the arms of the chair and tented his hands in front of his mouth and looked at me silently.

I said, "Good morning, Judge."

He nodded. I waited. He studied me some more. I leaned my chair back and put my feet up. He tapped his tented hands against his upper lip. I folded my hands and let them rest on my stomach.

"First," Ronan said, "I apologize for sending those two cretins to threaten you."

"They didn't threaten me very much," I said.

"They had once appeared before me in court. I

thought they were more formidable than apparently they were."

"Or I was more formidable."

Ronan nodded his head once. "Perhaps," he said. "In any case, it was uncalled for."

I had nothing to add to that so I kept quiet.

Ronan stood up suddenly and walked past me and looked out my window. Outside the window it was a hot day, and overcast, with a promise of rain later. Ronan stared out my window silently. I swiveled my chair so I could look at him while he looked out.

Finally, with his back to me and his gaze fixed on the world outside my window, he said, "Jeanette told me about the pictures."

"The ones from Sterling's apartment," I said.

"Yes."

"I'm sorry," I said.

"I have power. I have money. I have a national reputation," he said. "But I am twice Jeanette's age."

I didn't say anything. He was so still as he stood looking out my window that he could have been a cardboard cutout. His voice hardly seemed to come from him as he talked.

"And I love her."

"That's good," I said.

"I don't know if she loves me," he said. "But she likes me. And she doesn't want to leave me."

"Some people might call that love," I said.

"Whatever it is," Ronan said, "it will suffice."

He turned back from the window and went and sat in my client chair again. He made no eye contact with me.

"Needless to say, we will take no further action against your client."

"He'll be glad to hear that," I said.

If I can find him.

Ronan took a tan leather checkbook from the inside pocket of his seersucker jacket.

"And I wish to recompense you for your time and inconvenience."

"That won't be necessary," I said.

"I insist," Ronan said.

He leaned forward and opened the checkbook on his side of my desk and got out a fountain pen.

"You've done too much insisting in your life, Judge. It's one of your problems."

Ronan looked up. His expression was startled.

"My client is so far downhill by now his reputation is probably irrelevant," I said. "But if his reputation were relevant, the charge of sexual harassment would linger on him like a bad smell."

"I . . ."

"You would need to do more than write a check," I said.

"I . . . I was afraid," he said. "I found a love letter from him to Jeanette. I was terrified. But I confronted her and she said he meant nothing to her. That he had harassed her sexually and that this letter was just another example of it."

"And you couldn't wait to believe her."

He nodded.

"And maybe there was some sort of low-level doubt that you wanted to put aside," I said, "so being you, you decided to sue. That would make it official. Then it would have to be true."

Ronan was trying to look autocratic, but it was hard because his shoulders had slumped and he was having trouble looking at me.

"And I'll bet you told Jeanette that corroborating evidence would be useful. The testimony of other women he'd harassed."

He nodded.

"So Jeanette went out and got her friends in on it."

"They were just trying to be supportive," Ronan said.

"Why'd she tell you?" I said.

He started to speak, and paused, and thought about it a moment. "She said she couldn't live with the secret."

"Too bad," I said. "The way things are shaping up, she might have been able to."

"It is best to know," he said.

"That's the official view," I said.

"You don't agree?"

"Sometimes a secret kept causes pain for one," I said. "And a secret shared causes pain for two."

"She told me because she cared for me."

"Sure," I said. "That's probably it."

We were quiet for a time. Outside my office window the air was thickening. It was darker. No rain yet, but soon there'd be thunder in the distance.

"You won't accept my check?" Ronan said.

"No."

"Your client has disappeared?" Ronan said.

"Yes."

"If you find him, offer him my apology."

"He might prefer the check," I said.

forty-seven

LEE FARRELL CALLED me on Friday morning. Outside was bright sunshine, temperature about eighty-two, slight breeze. A perfect day to be outside. I was inside. I had nothing to do inside or outside. But I did it better inside. I didn't know where Sterling was. I didn't know if he'd killed Carla, or even Cony Brown for that matter. I had nowhere else to go, and no one to ask, and nothing to follow up. I was thrilled that the phone rang.

"Talked to Somerville half hour ago," Farrell said. "The gun you took away from Wechsler's shooter?"

"Philchock," I said.

"Yeah. Cambridge passed it over to Somerville and they fired couple rounds and compared them to the bullet that killed Carla Quagliozzi. No match."

"That's too bad," I said.

"On the other hand—it was Quirk's idea—we took the slugs from Carla and compared them to the one came out of Cony Brown, the guy got diced in Sterling's office?"

"And you got a match," I said.

"That's right."

"You noticed where this seems to be going," I said.

"It's beginning to look like Susan's ex," he said. "Lotta questions though."

"A lot," I said.

"You answer any of them, you'll call me," Farrell said.

"First thing," I said.

We hung up. I stood up and stared out my window for a while. I went over to the sink and got a drink of water. I stood for a time and looked at the picture of Jackie Robinson on my wall above the file cabinet. When I got through looking at Jackie, I went back and looked out the window some more. Then I put on my sunglasses and went out of the office and began to walk. After a while I ended up at the Harbor Health Club, in the boxing room, which Henry kept like a family secret in the back end of the club.

I hit the heavy bag for a while. It was the kind of repetitive, effortful, mindless endeavor that I seemed best qualified for. I dug left hooks into it, circled it, landing stiff jabs at will, going to the body hard and when the hands came down, delivering my crushing over-hand right. I stopped, took a breather, drank some water, and did it again. After an hour the bag was ready to say *no mas*, my hair was plastered to my skull, and my sweatshirt was soaked through. I took some steam, then a shower, and was dressed and admiring myself in the mirror when Henry came into the locker room.

"Am I better looking than Tom Cruise? Or what?"

"You're taller," Henry said. "Settle for that."

"Everybody's taller, for crissake."

"Almost everybody," Henry said. "Susan called. Said to tell you that Brad was visiting at her house."

I said, "Thank you," and walked past Henry and out through the health club.

The Central Artery was always problematic if you were in a hurry, and now that it was in the process of being disassembled and placed underground, it was less reliable than Dennis Rodman. I went up Atlantic Avenue as fast as the spillover from the Big Dig would let me. I went past the North Station on Causeway Street, deked down Lomansy Way, and went along Nashua Street past the Suffolk County Jail and the Spaulding Rehab Hospital. I ran the light at Leverett Circle, which annoyed several drivers, and I was loose and in an open field on Storrow Drive.

In one sense, Brad was Susan's problem. And Susan would, if given enough space, solve her own problems. On the other hand, Brad may have killed two people and while he probably was not as tough as Susan, he was a lot bigger. And she had called.

I pulled up in front of Susan's house twenty-one minutes after I had left the Harbor Health Club and parked and let myself in. The door to her waiting room was closed. I opened it and went in. There was a thin-faced woman reading a copy of *The New Yorker* in one of the waiting room chairs. She had rimless glasses and a pointy nose. The door to Susan's office was closed. The woman did not look up.

I said, "Excuse me, what time is your appointment?"

The woman looked at me as if I had proposed sodomy.

"Twelve-fifty," she said and returned huffily to studying "Talk of the Town."

It was 12:34. I sat in the chair opposite the door and waited. There was a white sound machine in one corner of the room and it hissed harmonically with the sound of conditioned air moving through the vents. Serenity. I looked at my watch. 12:35. I took some air in through my nose and let it out slowly. The sharp-nosed woman didn't look up from *The New Yorker*, but she managed through body language to convey how boorish she thought I was to breathe deeply this close to the sepulchre. At 12:52 the door to Susan's office opened and a square-jawed young man with longish hair came out, and made no eye contact with either me or Needle Nose. Susan was wearing a subdued gray suit. She saw me.

"Please come in, Adele," she said to Eagle Beak.

When Adele had put down her *New Yorker* and stalked into Susan's office, Susan said, "I'll be with you in a moment."

She closed the door and walked over to me.

"Pearl is with me in the office," Susan said. "Brad came this morning. He's upstairs. He said he had nowhere else to go. He said he was, quote, at his wit's end, unquote. He's unshaven. He appears exhausted. I think he's been sleeping in parks. When I left, he was asleep on my bed with all his clothes on."

"How would you like me to handle it?" I said.

"As you think best. Today is my short day. Adele is my final patient."

"I'll wait for you here," I said. "And we'll go up together."

"Fine," Susan said and turned back toward her office. With her hand on the doorknob she stopped for a moment and turned and looked at me.

"I'm all right with this," she said.

"Good," I said.

And she went into her office.

forty-eight

Susan's office was on the first floor of her house and her apartment was on the second. It was quarter to two when, with Adele stabilized for the weekend, and Pearl somewhat grumpily left behind on the couch in Susan's office, Susan and I went upstairs, and she unlocked her apartment door. There was a radio playing, and I could hear the shower running. Susan went to the kitchen and shut off the radio. Looking through Susan's open door I could see that the bathroom door was ajar. The shower stopped and after a moment the bathroom door opened a little wider.

"It's me," Susan said.

The door opened fully and Brad came out with a towel wrapped inexpertly around his waist. His hair was wet and he was clean shaven. His skin was pale and sort of inelastic looking, and the hair on his chest was gray, but he hadn't gotten fat. He saw me and jumped about six inches. Not a bad vertical leap for a white Harvard guy.

"Jesus Christ," he said. "It's you."

"Yes it is," I said.

"You startled me," he said. "Lucky I had this towel on."

"Get dressed," I said.

"You bet," he said. "Suze, can you rustle me up a little grub? I'm totally famished."

He went into Susan's bedroom and closed the door. Susan was still in the kitchen.

"I didn't know you rustled up grub," I said.

"I don't."

"I'll make some coffee," I said.

"Fine."

Susan sat on a stool at her kitchen counter and watched me assemble the coffee and water in Mr. Coffee. When it was ready, I poured us each a cup.

"Didn't you leave some Irish whisky here last year?" she said.

"Yes."

"I'll have some in my coffee," she said.

I found the whisky in the cabinet above the refrigerator and poured some into her cup.

"Thank you," she said.

I put some milk and sugar in my coffee and leaned my hips on the counter next to the refrigerator. Brad came into the kitchen, barefoot, wearing a tee shirt and a pair of jeans. The tee shirt hung loose outside the jeans.

"I smell java," he said.

"In the pot on the counter," I said.

He poured some.

"Milk and sugar?"

"Nope, I like it black as the devil's soul, and lots of it," he said. "These are your duds, I assume."

"Yes."

"Pants are a tad short," he said.

"Tee shirt's kind of loose around the chest and arms too," I said.

Susan smiled and sipped her coffee.

"Any chow?" he said.

"There's some eggs in the refrigerator," Susan said.

"Suze, come on, I don't really cook very well."

"Me either."

"No? I figured you'd learned by now."

"Never did," Susan said. "Never wanted to."

"Damn," Brad said. "I'm really hungry."

Neither of us said anything. Brad opened a few cabinet doors randomly and found some rye bread, and a half jar of peanut butter.

"For shame," I said to Susan.

"Only keep it for guests," she said to me.

"You don't have any white bread, do you?"

"No."

"Jelly?"

"Refrigerator."

He found some boysenberry jam in the refrigerator and looked at it the way Macbeth had looked at the spot.

"What kind is this?"

"Boysenberry," Susan said.

"Well, it'll have to do," Brad said. "Got something to make a sandwich?"

"Knife is in the left drawer in front of you," Susan said.

She took another sip of her coffee. Her face was contemplative. She looked as if she had just awakened from a deep refreshing sleep and was waiting to see what the day would bring. Brad made an amateurish-looking peanut butter and jelly sandwich and ate it rapidly, hunched over the counter with swallows of coffee in between bites. As soon as he had finished, he made another one. This one was no better looking but it lasted longer. Susan and I were quiet while he ate.

"Sorry to be stowing it away like this," Brad said, "but I am really famished."

He finished his second sandwich and went to the sink to rinse his hands and face. I could see that he had a small gun in his right hip pocket. I took mine off my hip and put it on the counter top and rested my right hand on it, shielded discretely by the refrigerator. Brad dried his hands and face on a paper towel and refilled his cup and came to the counter where we sat and leaned his forearms on it.

"Wow," he said. "Nothing like getting inside a shower and outside of some strong Joe to make you feel brand new."

"So where have you been?" Susan said.

"Round and about," Brad said. "I ran out of money three four days ago."

"And you came to me," Susan said. "Do you think I'll give you money?"

"I had nowhere else to go, Suzie-Q."

"Why didn't you go home?" Susan said.

Her voice was calm and pleasant and implacable. Occasionally she raised her coffee cup with both hands and took a sip.

"We're maybe not married anymore, sure, but hell, we're still family."

"No, Brad, we're not family. That's what divorce means."

"We meant something to one another, Suzuki. We meant quite a lot."

"Brad, think about this for a moment. There was a reason why I divorced you."

"Well, sure, I made some mistakes."

"We both did, but finally after all that is taken into account, and to oversimplify a little perhaps, for effect, there's more to it than that: I divorced you because I didn't like you."

Brad straightened as if he'd been stuck with a pin. He frowned and opened his mouth and closed it and opened it again and said, "I can't believe you said that."

"One of the biggest problems you have, Brad," Susan said, "is you can only believe what you want to or need to. I didn't like you. I don't like you. The first time you came to see me I thought you were asking for help and I felt enough guilt to try to get you help."

"Him?" Brad said.

"Now I realize you were asking me for money," Susan said. "But I was not sufficiently, ah, evolved, and I misunderstood. I tried to save you."

"By sending me him? Thanks a lot."

"It was my mistake and it is my responsibility that he's involved with you. But I'm not going to compound that mistake by lying to you or to myself."

"What are you saying?"

"I'm saying that when you have finished your coffee and we're through talking, you'll have to leave."

"And go where?"

"Probably to hell."

"And you don't care?"

"You'll get there anyway," Susan said. "Whatever I do."

"That's cold, Sue, that's really cold."

"Yes," she said.

"I'm just trying to stay alive, Susie."

"I wish you success," Susan said.

"And what happens if I won't leave? Your bully boy throws me out?"

I smiled courteously.

"You'll have to leave," Susan said.

"Well, let me tell you right, damned, now, Suzie Qu-sie, I've dealt with tougher guys than him."

"There's no need to put it to the test," Susan said. "I'll simply call the police."

"Susan, for God's sake, I can't let the cops find me. If I have to leave here, I've got no place to go. If they find me, they'll kill me."

"The cops?"

"Of course not."

"Who?"

She said it so gently, and it slipped into the flow of the argument so easily that Brad answered it before he knew he'd been asked.

"Wechsler and Gavin," he said in the exasperated tone one uses to explain the obvious to an idiot. Susan was looking at him over the rim of her cup. She sipped a little of the whisky-laced coffee and then slowly lowered the cup, and sat back a little.

"Why?"

"Why, for crissake . . ."

In mid-sentence Brad realized that he had said too much. He stopped and shut his mouth and his face had a set look to it.

"Why are Gavin and Wechsler after you?"

Brad shook his head. Susan was silent, waiting. Brad tried to match her silence but he couldn't.

"They think I got something they want," he said.

"What?"

Brad clamped his mouth shut and shook his head.

Susan waited. Brad shook his head. Susan looked at me.

"Would you like to contribute?" she said.

"It's a blue floppy disk," I said. "For a computer."

"Shut up," Brad said.

"What's on the disk?" Susan said.

Brad shook his head. Susan looked at me.

"I'd guess it was the record of his scam with Gavin," I said, "and indirectly, Wechsler."

"Is that right?" Susan said to Brad.

"Of course not," Brad said. "But you'll probably believe him anyway."

"I probably will," Susan said. "Go ahead."

"This is how I think it went," I said to Brad. "Feel free to correct me. I think you were looking for money and, being the way you are, you went to Carla Quagliozzi, your ex-wife, and tried to get some. She wouldn't give you any, but she sent you to her boyfriend, Richard Gavin, who is Haskell Wechsler's lawyer."

"I don't have to stand around here and listen to this tripe," Brad said to Susan.

"No," Susan said, "you don't."

"Gavin arranged for you to borrow some money from Haskell," I said, "and of course you couldn't pay it back, and of course you got behind on the interest. Maybe Gavin expected that. Maybe Gavin baited you with the loan so they could squeeze you later. I don't know how clever he is."

Brad tried looking out the window as if he were bored.

"But I know how clever you are," I said. "So after they threatened you enough to scare you, they made you a proposition. Haskell accumulates a lot of cash, being a loan shark, and he needed to launder it. You run fund-raising events. So they'd finance the fund-raisers, like Galapalooza, and you would then donate their costs, plus maybe a little extra for your vig, back to them through a dummy charity called Civil Streets."

"See." Brad said. "See, Susan, how he is? If what he said was true, then Gavin and Wechsler would love me. Why would they be after me?"

"Because you, being you, skimmed on them. You were supposed to pay off the other charities too, to make it look right. But you didn't. From Galapalooza you gave them what you agreed to, but you kept the rest, and stiffed the other charities."

"You were supposed to be helping me with that harassment case," Brad said. "How come you been snooping around in my other business?"

"It fell in my lap," I said. "And I admit I stirred it up a bit, and maybe because I did, Gavin found out that you were cheating on the other charities. But it would have happened sooner or later. The charity groups talk to each other. Anyway, Gavin looked into it himself and was very unhappy to find that you'd cheated everyone else, because it meant sooner or later someone would complain and the AG's office would look into it, and everybody's fat would be in the fire."

"Suze, do you believe all this?" Brad said.

"Yes."

"Well, I suppose you would, wouldn't you," he said.

"So Gavin sent over a guy he'd once represented, guy named Cony Brown, to persuade you to cough up the money you'd skimmed. And of course you couldn't because you didn't have it, because you spent it as soon as you got it. And Cony got aggressive and you shot him, and took the disk—I assume you figured it would protect you if they didn't know where it was—and you scooted."

"I should have sent you packing," Brad said, "the minute she sent you to me."

"I probably hurried things along," I said. "But you'd have gotten yourself into this rat's alley anyway."

"What I don't understand," Susan said, "the sexual harassment suit really started the unraveling of this whole thing. Why didn't you just show the pictures of Jeanette to her husband It would have stopped him in his tracks."

"I don't kiss and tell," Brad said.

"Chivalry?" Susan said.

"Whatever you think of me," Brad said, "there are things I believe in."

Susan looked at me. I shrugged.

"Hitler liked dogs," I said.

"What the hell's that supposed to mean," Brad said.

"People are inconsistent," I said.

"Then why in heaven's name did you let him in?" Susan said.

I knew the "him" was me. Neither one of them seemed able to use my name. I wasn't sure why, but I didn't mind.

"To humor you."

"You think?" Susan said to me.

"Maybe there was a little more," I said. "Maybe he hoped that I would find him in such serious need of cash that you would relent and open your heart and your coffers."

Susan nodded.

"And he was probably scared. Gavin and Wechsler would have leaned on him pretty hard before they set him up in the fund-raiser scam. He might have thought a, ah, bully boy would be useful."

"And he would have thought he could manipulate you," Susan said. "And he would have assumed that you would protect him because of me."

"Which I will," I said.

"No," Susan said. "You won't."

The kitchen was quiet except for the soft white sound of air conditioning. I let my gun rest against my right thigh. Cony Brown was a pro and Brad had cranked him.

"So," Sterling said, "you are prepared to throw me to the wolves? Both of you?"

He looked hard at Susan. She had one last sip of her strong coffee and put the cup down and folded her hands behind it on the counter top. She looked back at Sterling.

Then she said to me, her eyes still on Sterling, "Do you think he killed Carla Quagliozzi?"

"Yes."

"And . . . cut out her tongue?"

"Yes."

Something happened to Sterling's face. Something stirred behind his eyes that changed the way he looked. Something repellent peeked out through the bland Ivy League disguise. It was nameless, and base, and it wasn't human. We both saw it. Perhaps Susan had seen it as often in her work. She didn't flinch.

She said, "You did that, didn't you, Brad."

The thing darted in and out of sight behind his eyes. He didn't speak. Susan got up from the counter and walked around it and stood in front of Sterling.

"You killed that woman and cut her tongue out," she said. "Didn't you."

The kitchen was cool and still. I could feel the trapezius muscles on top of my shoulders begin to bunch. I took in some air and made them relax. When Sterling finally spoke it was shocking. His voice came out in an eerily adolescent whine.

"What was I supposed to do?" he said. "They send some gangster to hurt me and I have to shoot him and the cops are after me. And I'm desperate. And down on my luck, for cripes sake, and go to her for help and she won't help. She says she's going to tell."

"Tell the police?" Susan said gently.

"Yes. Because of him."

I knew he meant me. So did Susan.

"He kept coming around, and then the cops, and she was going to go there and tell on me."

"To the police?" Susan said. "She was going to the police?"

"Yes."

Tears had formed in Sterling's eyes.

"She was my wife, for cripes sake. She was supposed to help me."

"So you had to kill her?" Susan said.

"I was supposed to let her tell?"

"And the . . . tongue," Susan said.

"So they'd know."

The sound of his voice had lost all hint of the man from whom it came. It sounded like a drill bit binding in metal.

"They'd know what?"

"That she was going to tell on us, so I had to kill her. It was a, a symbol. So they'd know I was protecting all of us."

"They being Gavin and Wechsler?"

" 'Course."

Susan looked at me.

"What did you use?" I said.

"My jackknife. My father always said a man was no better than the knife he carried. I always carry a good jackknife."

"And what did you do with it?"

"With what?"

"The tongue," I said.

"The thing in the sink, you know . . ." He made a grinding noise.

"Disposal," Susan said.

"Yuh, disposal." He gestured down, with his forefinger.

Susan stared at him for a moment with no expression on her face, then she turned and walked back and stood next to me. The counter was between Sterling and us. He looked a little dazed.

"What was I supposed to do," he said. "Everybody I turn to lets me down."

Susan took a deep breath and let it out and walked to the end of the counter and picked up the phone.

"No," Sterling said.

He put his right hand behind him, feeling for the gun in his back pocket. I brought mine up from beside my thigh and aimed it at the middle of his chest.

"Try to use the gun and I'll kill you," I said.

Sterling froze in mid gesture. He looked at Susan.

"Take the gun out slowly, hold it with your thumb and forefinger only, and put it on the counter in front of me. And step back away from it."

The thing in behind his eyes was seething now. He didn't want to give up the gun. He wanted to kill both of us and everyone else who wouldn't help him. But the thing didn't make him blind. Maybe he saw something in my eyes. Maybe he knew that shooting him would satisfy me in ways that few things could. Slowly and carefully he took the gun out and put it on the counter. It was a Targa .380. He still seemed dazed. I picked the gun up and stuck it in my belt.

"Susie," he said. "For God's sake, Susie."

Susan dialed 911.

"I'm not going to stay here," he said. "You can shoot me if you want."

I shook my head. And he turned and walked from the kitchen. I followed him. He went through the living room to the hall and out the apartment door, down the stairway, and out the front door of the building. The door swung shut and latched gently behind him. From the front hall window I watched him run in the late afternoon sunshine under the filtering trees, up Linnaean Street toward Mass Ave.

Susan came to stand beside me. She put her forehead against the wall beside the window and closed her eyes.

"My God," she said. "My God."

I stood beside her without touching her, and we stood like that until the cops came.

forty-nine

SUSAN AND I sat across from each other in her kitchen with a bottle of Irish whisky on the counter between us and no lights on. Pearl had been liberated from the office and tended to, and was lying on the couch in the living room. The cops were gone. The sun was down, and the early evening had taken on a bluish tint outside the kitchen windows.

"What will happen to him?" Susan said.

"Brad? They'll catch him."

"You seem so sure."

"He's too dumb," I said. "He won't last long."

"Can they prove he did what you said he did?"

"Well, they've got his gun. It should match up with the slugs they took out of Cony Brown and Carla."

"How awful . . . the tongue especially."

"I know," I said. "Funny thing. It was supposed to reassure Gavin and Wechsler. I don't think Wechsler even noticed it had happened. This was mostly Gavin and Brad, I think. But Gavin took it as a threat. You know, *keep quiet or this will happen to you*. He was walking around with bodyguards."

"You don't think Wechsler was involved?"

"He was involved," I said, "but basically just to have his money laundered. I don't think he even knew the mechanics."

"Because of the way he acted when you confronted him?"

"Yes."

"And you trust your instincts?"

"Have to," I said. "Most of the actually important clues in this business are really how people are. If you can't read human behavior pretty good after a while, you never get very good at this."

"But human behavior doesn't get you a conviction. You have to have hard evidence."

"True," I said. "But the behavior tells you where to look, or, sometimes, what to manufacture."

"Manufacture?"

"Cops do it. I'm not saying it's right, but they know somebody did a thing and can't prove it, so they manufacture something that will prove it."

"If they catch Brad, do you think he'll implicate Gavin and Wechsler?"

"You saw him tonight. He'd implicate his mother," I said.

"And if they don't catch him? Can you prove anything against the other two?"

I smiled. It was my moment. I took a small blue computer disk out of my shirt pocket and held it up.

"It was in your bedroom, under some sweaters," I said. "I knew he'd have it with him, and if he didn't have it in his pocket, it had to be here someplace."

"When did you find it?"

"While you were freeing Pearl from the office," I said.

"And you didn't give it to the police?"

"I want to look at it first," I said. "If it's what I think it is, I'll give it to them tomorrow."

"And if it is what you think it is, it will convict them."

"Yes," I said.

I put the disk back in my shirt pocket.

"So you've got them all," Susan said.

"I think so," I said.

Susan raised her glass and I touched the rim of mine to hers. We were quiet. The blue light had darkened as the evening drifted toward night. The whisky made my stomach warm. I could feel myself loosen slowly. Sometimes the only way I knew I was tense was feeling not tense afterwards. Susan took a short drink of whisky and let it slide down her throat and looked at me with her eyes simultaneously dark and bright. I wondered how she did that.

"You were careful of me when Brad was here," Susan said.

She had a finger of whisky in the bottom of a short thick glass and she swirled it a little as she talked.

"Yeah?"

"You stepped back as much as you could," she said. "You let me do it."

"Who better?" I said.

"You know what I mean. You didn't demean me by protecting me."

"This wasn't about me," I said.

"Well, the thing is, of course, that it was about you too. It was about what a fool I was to think I could help Brad. And, of course, my idea of helping him was to ask you to do it."

I took two ice cubes from a bowl on the counter and

dropped them into my glass and splashed a swallow or so of whisky on it. I looked at Susan's glass and she shook her head.

"I like it when I can help you," I said.

"But to ask you to help my ex-husband, whom, since you have the most normal emotional responses of anyone I know, you'd have preferred to drown . . ." She shook her head. "Did you want to shoot him when you had the chance?"

"You bet," I said.

"You could have shot him when he reached for his gun. It would have been self-defense. No one, me included, could have faulted you."

"I know."

"So why didn't you?"

"If I shot everybody I wanted to," I said, "I'd go broke buying ammunition."

Susan swished her whisky some more and took a sip of it and held the glass up and looked at the early evening light through it. Then she put it back on the counter.

"So why didn't you?" she said.

"Well, I try not to kill people I don't have to," I said.

"I understand that. But I have also seen you very aggressive with people who have only been mildly disrespectful to me. There was none of that here."

"No."

"You stayed out of it as much as you could."

"Yes."

"Because the only way for me to come out of this without feeling like a perfect jerk was to confront him myself, and be the one to decide what to do."

"I think *perfect jerk* is a bit harsh."

She shook her head impatiently. "And you let me do

that as much as you could, knowing he had already killed two people."

"Seemed a good idea at the time," I said.

"But how do you know? How can you know things like that? A man like you."

I loved her seriousness. I loved that she was serious about me. And that we were talking intensely about me. I was having a very good time.

"I learned a lot of what I know from you," I said.

"That's a lovely thing to say."

"It's true," I said.

"And I've learned a great deal from you," she said.

"We stick with each other long enough, and we may get smart as hell," I said.

Susan reached out with her left hand and took hold of mine. We sat across from each other and held hands and drank our whisky. It was dark now. I could barely see her across from me. But I could feel her intangible energy.

After a while Susan said, "Even if we don't."

And after another while I said, "Even if."

And then we were perfectly quiet, nearly invisible in the dark.

OUTSIDE MY WINDOW a mixture of rain and snow was settling into slush on Berkeley Street. I was listening to a spring training game from Florida between the Sox and the Blue Jays. Joe Castiglione and Jerry Trupiano were calling the game and struggling bravely to read all the drop-ins the station had sold. They did as well as anyone could, but Red Barber and Mel Allen would have had trouble with the number of commercials these guys had to slip in. The leisurely pace of baseball had once been made for radio. It allowed the announcers to talk about baseball in perfect consonance with the rhythm of the game. We listened not only to hear what happened but because we liked the music of it. The sound of a late game from the coast, between two teams out of contention on a Sunday afternoon in August, driving home from the beach. The crowd noise was faint in the background, the voices of the play-by-play guys embroidering on a dull game. Now there was little time for baseball talk. There was barely time for play-by-play. And much of the music was gone. Still, it was the sound of spring, and it took some of the chill out of the slush storm.

Just after the fifth inning started, Hawk came into my office with a smallish man in a short haircut, wearing a dark three-piece suit and a red and white polka dot bow tie. His skin was blue black and seemed tight on him. I turned the radio down, but not off.

"Client," Hawk said.

"Ever hopeful," I said.

I recognized the small man. His name was Robinson Nevins. He was a professor at the university, the author of at least a dozen books, a frequent guest on television shows, and a nationally known figure in what the press calls The Black Community. *Time* magazine had once referred to him as "the Lion of Academe."

"I'm Robinson Nevins," he said and put his hand out. I leaned forward and shook it without getting up. "Hawk may be premature in calling me a client. We need to talk a bit first, among other things we ought to find out if we can get along."

"Whose tab?" I said to Hawk.

"Guarantee half everything I get," Hawk said.

"That much," I said.

"I can't afford very much," Nevins said.

"Maybe we won't get along," I said.

"I am dependent largely on a university salary and, as I'm sure you know, that is not a handsome sum."

"Depends what sums you're used to," I said. "How about the books?"

"The books are well received, and have influence I hope beyond their sales. Their sales are modest. I make some money on the lecture circuit, but far too often I speak because I feel the cause is just rather than the price is right."

"Don't you hate when that happens," I said.

Nevins smiled, but not as if he thought I was funny.

"What would you like to pay me a modest amount to do?" I said.

"I have been denied tenure," Nevins said.

I stared at him.

"Tenure?" I said.

"Yes. Unjustly."

"And you want me to look into that?" I said.

"Yes."

"Tenure," I said.

"Yes."

I was silent. Nevins didn't say anything else. I looked at Hawk.

"You want me to do this?" I said to Hawk.

"Yes."

I was silent again.

"I understand your reaction," Nevins said. "I sound churlish to you. And you think that there are causes of greater urgency than whether I get tenure at the university."

I pointed a finger at Nevins. "Bingo," I said.

"I know, were I you that would be my reaction. But it is not simply that I am denied tenure and therefore will have to leave. I can find another job. What is at issue here is that I shouldn't have been denied tenure. I am more qualified than most members of the tenure committee. More qualified than many who have received tenure."

"You think it's racial?" I said.

"It would be an easy supposition and one most of us have made correctly in our lives," Nevins said. "But I am, in fact, not sure that it is."

"What else?" I said.

"I don't know. I am something of an anomaly for a black man at the university. I am relatively conservative."

"What do you teach?"

"American literature."

"Black perspective?"

"Well, my perspective. I include black writers, but I also include a number of dead white men."

"Daring," I said.

"Do you know that we are turning out English Ph.Ds who have never read Milton?"

"I didn't know that," I said. "You think you were shot down for being insufficiently correct?"

"Possibly," Nevins said. "I don't know. What I know is there was a smear campaign orchestrated by someone, which I believe cost me tenure."

"You want me to find out who did the smearing?"

"Yes."

I looked at Hawk again. He nodded.

"Wouldn't an attorney be more likely to get you your tenure?"

"I am not fighting this because I didn't get tenure. I'm fighting this because it's wrong."

"If you got the tenure decision reversed, would you accept it?"

Nevins smiled at the question.

"You press a person, don't you," he said.

"I like to know things," I said.

"Like how sincere I am about fighting this because it's wrong."

"That would be good to know," I said.

"If I were offered tenure I would have to assess my options. But even if I accepted it, the process was still wrong."

"What was the thrust of the smear campaign?"

Hawk appeared to be listening to the faintly audible ball game. And he was. If asked he could give you the score and recap the last inning. He would also be able to tell you everything I said or Nevins said and how we looked when we said it.

"A young man, a graduate student, committed suicide this past semester. It was alleged to be the result of a sexual relationship with me."

"What was his name?" I said.

"Prentice Lamont."

"Any truth to it?"

"None."

I nodded.

"I imagine you'd like that laid to rest as well."

"Yes."

"Okay," I said.

"Okay meaning you'll do it?"

"Yep."

Nevins seemed mildly puzzled.

"Like that?"

"Yep."

"Aren't you going to ask if I'm gay?"

"Nope."

"Why not?"

"Don't care."

"But," Nevins frowned, "it might be germane."

"If it is, I'll ask," I said.

Nevins opened his mouth and closed it and sat back in his chair. Then he took a green-covered checkbook out of his inside coat pocket.

"What will you need for a retainer?"

"No need for a retainer," I said.

"Oh, but I insist. I don't want favors."

Hawk was looking out the window at the slush accumulating around the stylishly booted ankles of the young women leaving the insurance companies on their way to lunch.

Without turning around he said, "He doing me a favor, Robinson."

Nevins was not slow. He looked once at Hawk, and back at me, and nodded to himself. He put the green checkbook back inside his coat and stood.

"Do you need anything else right now?" he said.

"No. I'll poke around at it, see what develops."

"And I'll hear from you?"

"Yes," I said.

"Will you be involved, Hawk?"

Hawk turned from the window and grinned at Nevins.

"Sure," he said. "I'll help him with the hard stuff."

Nevins put out his hand. "I appreciate your taking this," he said, "for whomever you're doing the favor."

I shook it.

"You need a ride anyplace?" he said to Hawk.

Hawk shook his head. Nevins nodded as if to confirm something in his head, and turned and left. Hawk continued to look out the window. The ball game had moved quietly into the eighth inning. Outside my window it was mostly rain now. Hawk turned away from the window and looked at me without expression.

"Tenure?" I said.

Hawk smiled.

" 'Fraid so," he said.

ROBERT B.PARKER
TROUBLE IN PARADISE

PUTNAM